ROSS

Riding Hard, Book 5

JENNIFER ASHLEY

JA/AG Publishing

Chapter One

❧

"I've got a stranded motorist on Fairpoint Road," Ross said into his radio as he pulled to the grassy side of the deserted highway. Rain pounded on his SUV's roof, and he raised his voice to hear himself. "Stopping to assist."

"Roger that," the tones of Mildred, River County's dispatcher, crackled through. "Need backup?"

"Nah, I got this."

Fairpoint was Farm Road 231 B, a lonely stretch between Riverbend and White Fork. The car, silver, had plowed through the mud on the shoulder and now was stuck half into and half out of the water-filled ditch, courtesy of the late May rainstorm. The car was sleek and looked expensive, probably a Mercedes, obscured by sheets of rain.

"Noted," Mildred said. "Oh, Ross, your mom called. She wants to know if you're home for supper tonight."

"Ha." Ross shifted on the seat. "Means she wants me to cook. If she calls back, tell her sure, I'll be there."

"You're a good boy, Ross."

"That's what they all say."

Mildred, a large woman comfortable with her weight,

whose hair color changed bi-weekly, laughed, signed off, and the radio went silent.

The license plate was from Texas, and the car was in fact a Mercedes, Ross saw as he halted behind it, low-slung and sporty. He didn't recognize the vehicle as belonging to a local, which meant the motorist could be from anywhere in the vast state. The rain was too bad for him to make out the tags or a city named on the plate holder. One back tire was flat.

As Ross set his brake, the driver's side door of the silver car opened, kicked by a foot in a white slipper. A leg in a pale stocking followed, accompanied by yards and yards of white tulle.

Ross knew it was called tulle from the four weddings he'd been to in the last year or so—one for each of his older Campbell brothers. The wives and wives-to-be had camped out in the living room at Circle C for months and talked about dresses and place settings and floral arrangements until Ross's eyes had glazed over. His brothers had watched their ladies with goofy looks on their faces.

The rest of the skirt came out of the car, followed by a satin bodice hugging a nicely shaped body. The woman's arms were bare, as was her head, her hair in a perfectly formed bun studded with tiny white flowers.

The young woman wrestled with the dress until she popped free of the car, then she brought up a cell phone and raised it high, her mouth moving in words Ross couldn't hear.

Pouring rain misted around her, deflating the skirts and darkening the bodice. Ross jumped out of his SUV at the same moment the woman spun and kicked the flat tire with one delicate slipper.

She let out a yell as her foot connected with the hard tire, then she hopped, slipped, and started to fall.

Ross caught her.

Warm, soft woman moved under his fingertips, lighting fire

in his blood. The silk let him feel her supple waist, a curve beneath his hand.

She had glitter in her hair, sparkling in what little light leaked through the clouds. Glitter also filmed her cheeks, which was cut by rivulets of mascara.

Blue eyes peered at Ross from behind the smeared mascara, giving her the look of a startled raccoon. Her nose was slightly crooked, lips brushed with pink. Below the turned-down mouth was a rounded chin, a suntanned neck, and more shoulders and bust than should be exposed in a hell of a rainstorm on a Texas back road.

Her hair was a light shade of brown or a dark shade of blond, dark and light strands blending into one another. The glitter was dissolving, and the white flowers drooped, rain plastering them to her head.

Ross recognized her with a jolt.

Callie Jones.

The beautiful, highborn, debutante Callie, who'd been the object of high-school Ross's fantasies. He'd crushed on her since the day he'd seen her next to his locker, talking to her friends, her curvy body outlined by a tight-sleeved top with glitter on it. She liked glitter.

When he'd swaggered up, a full-of-himself Campbell, and said, "Pardon me, ladies," she'd flashed him a smile that had kept him awake for a week.

Callie wasn't smiling now, and it was doubtful she remembered him from their few and brief encounters. She'd been a grade higher than he was, and their paths hadn't crossed much —not at all once she'd graduated and left Riverbend.

Now she was back in River County, stuck in a storm ... in a wedding dress.

"Easy," was Ross's great opening line. "Bad day to break your toes."

"You think?" The outraged voice that came over the driving rain managed to maintain some sultry tones.

Callie's exposed skin had risen in goose bumps, and the silk of the dress was already sodden. Much longer and a thousand dollars' worth of wedding gown would be a melted rag.

Ross took a firm grip on her elbow and guided her up the slippery grass and mud bank to his SUV, where he opened the passenger door. She struggled with the high step and all the tulle, and Ross assisted with a professional hand to her side.

The warmth of her pulled at him, and his hand splayed across her waist before he could stop it. All he had to do was slide his other hand to her back, pull her a little closer, and brush those pink, parted lips …

Callie met his gaze, and her eyes widened the slightest bit.

This woman was churning with rage, burning bright with it. She clenched her jaw and balled her hands, jerking herself from his touch and sliding onto the seat.

Ross stuffed tulle around her feet … and stuffed and stuffed. The dress was massive.

Callie gathered it up, piling it on her lap until she was one big puffball, her wet bodice and glittery head poking from the cloud. Her breasts rose over the neckline with her sharp breath. If she breathed any harder, she'd pop right out of the gown.

Hell of a picture. Ross shut the door and stepped back into the rain to let its harsh chill cut the sudden heat inside him. He couldn't believe he was lusting after a rain-drenched Callie, who was obviously about to marry someone *else*.

No, he could believe it. Callie was hotter than ever, and her groom was one lucky guy.

Ross wasn't ashamed of his attraction to women—what he did *because* of that attraction would make him either a good guy or an asshole. Ross could admire a beautiful woman but walk away, no harm, no foul. He'd had plenty of girlfriends since he'd started going out at age sixteen, and he wasn't desperate for affection. He was the youngest Campbell, the cute one, the one with the four famous stunt-riding older brothers. Teenaged Ross had milked that for all he was worth.

He wiped rain out of his face as he rounded the SUV and climbed into the driver's seat.

"Hang tight," he told the ball of wet fabric beside him. "I'll call a tow."

"I can't wait for a *tow*." Callie banged frustrated fists into the netting. "If you hadn't noticed, I have someplace to be. Can't we just change the tire?"

We, as though she'd be out there shoving a jack under the car.

Impolite to laugh at her, but Ross did it anyway. "That pretty car of yours is stuck, ma'am. I can't haul it out of the ditch with my bare hands."

"Don't you have a rope or anything? And I'm not a *ma'am*. Shit, I'm not even married yet."

"Well, if I called you honey, or sweetheart, I'm guessing you'd smack me upside the head. Or report me. Sheriff Hennessy already doesn't like me, so there would go my job. Let's stick with ma'am."

"Or you could call me Callie," she said. "Callie Jones." Before Ross could respond she said, "Yes, I'm one of those 'Jones girls'." She did finger quotes, sounding weary.

"Ross Campbell. We went to the same high school."

"I know we did. I recognize you." The corners of her lips twitched, a tiny smile breaking through her anger. "You're one of those 'Campbell boys.'" She repeated the finger quotes.

"Yep." Ross flashed her a grin. "But not the famous ones. I got a real job."

"Instead of falling off horses for a living?" Callie's tone turned wistful. "I'd love to be able to ride like your brothers do."

"You ride?"

"I grew up on a ranch in the middle of Texas with a father who rides every day—I didn't have a choice. But yeah, I love it. Haven't had much of a chance these days." She shook a fold of her skirt. "Been a little busy. What am I going to do, Mr. Campbell?"

"Ross. If you don't call me mister, I won't call you ma'am. Deal?"

"Deal." She held out her hand, and Ross enveloped it with his.

Again with the fire. Ross didn't jerk away, because that would signal his reaction, the one that made him want to hold on and not let go.

The Jones girls—the three daughters of Caleb Jones, the richest man in River County, who owned a couple hundred sections of land and ran vast herds of cattle—were untouchable. *Way out of your league, dude,* was the remark to any male in Riverbend High School who even looked at a Jones.

Callie had been worth losing sleep over. Even now, wet as a half-drowned rat, her eyes ringed with black, her wet netting musty, she was amazing. The warmth of her was electric, even through a friendly handshake.

Ross made himself release her and reach for his radio.

"I'll drive you where you need to go. Let me get Sanchez over here to babysit your car, so some opportunistic car thief doesn't swim out and take it."

"I can't even wait for that. I'm already late, and I bet Devon's shitting a brick. He has a thing about punctuality."

Ross looked at her in surprise. "Well, if he doesn't think you're worth waiting for, he's an idiot."

"Aw." The twitch of lips turned into a wide smile, which flushed her cheeks. "That's sweet."

"Sweet. Yeah, that's me. Don't worry, ma'am—I mean, Callie. I'll get you to the church ... maybe not on time. But a bride's supposed to make an entrance, right? I have four sisters-in-law. I've walked so many bridesmaids up the aisle, it's not funny."

Another fleeting smile. "Always a groomsman, never a groom?"

"Not if I can help it." Ross clicked on the radio as the rain chose that moment to pick up again. "Mildred, where's Sanchez?"

Static. "East 2432 last time he checked in."

"Good. He's only a couple miles away. Tell him to haul ass to the fourth mile marker on Fairpoint to watch over a silver Mercedes, Texas license plate ..." He glanced at Callie who told him the numbers and letters in her low-pitched voice. A plate number had never sounded so sexy.

Ross repeated it to Mildred. "Wake up K.D. and tell him to bring his tow to the same spot. Take it to his garage, fix the flat, and the owner will pick it up later."

"Roger all that. Where are you going to be, Ross?"

"Church. Got a wedding to get to. Over and out."

"What?" Mildred spluttered as Ross hung up the radio. "Ross Campbell ..."

Ross clicked it off, put the SUV in gear, and sped onto the road, tires spinning in the mud.

CALLIE FOUGHT FURY, NAUSEA, HYSTERICAL LAUGHTER, AND nausea again. Of all the stupid days for a tire to go flat, for it to rain, for her car to slide off the road with a blowout, it had to be this one. All because her sisters couldn't be trusted to remember one stupid thing—pick up the bride.

"I'm late for everything in my life." Rain pounded on the windshield, too fast for the SUV's wipers to clear it. "It's kind of a joke. I told myself that this time—this *one* time, I wasn't going to screw up." She poked the air. "Trina—my best friend —offered to drive me, but oh, no, I said. My sisters and me, we should do this together. So what do they do? Leave me in the dust. I'm gonna kill them." Callie shot Ross a glance. "Oh, maybe I shouldn't say that to a cop."

He grinned at her, the wide smile that lit up his sun-bronzed face and made his eyes sparkle. Ross Campbell had been good-looking enough when they'd been kids. That boy from years ago had filled out into a man, and holy crap, what a man.

Devon was handsome too, in an always-wears-a-suit, stock-broker kind of way. Ross, in contrast, was salt-of-the-earth Texas—not afraid of its sun and wind, if the tanned arm between his khaki short sleeves and strong hands was anything to go by. The sun had left creases around his eyes, which were framed by black lashes as dark as the hair on his head. He'd buzzed his hair short, giving him a military look that matched the sharply creased uniform, now dark with rain.

His eyes were his best feature. Deep blue, like bluebonnets. Callie doubted any man wanted to be compared to a flower, but that's what he made her think of—the bluebonnets that carpeted the Hill Country fields in spring.

He was talking in a rumbling voice touched with a Central Texas accent. "I get what you mean. I have four brothers. And I'm deputy, not a cop."

"Is there a difference?"

"Don't get me started. And why are you all decked out already? I thought brides got dressed at the church."

Callie let her hands drop into the cushion of tulle. "My sisters again. One of them was supposed to help me dress and drive me in. The hairdresser got me into the gown, then she had to go to her next appointment, and I'm waiting, waiting. Finally, I said, screw it, I can drive myself. My car was right outside the front door. All I had to do was get in, head to the church, and run inside. I don't know what the hell blew my tire, and my cell phone couldn't find a signal. But it doesn't matter—I can't wait for roadside service. Vows to say, honey-moons to go on." She caught sight of the time on Ross's dashboard and groaned. The ceremony should have started half an hour ago.

She knew Ross couldn't drive any faster. The rain was coming down so hard that visibility was nil. Ross had to inch his way through the downpour.

"Who you marrying?" he asked conversationally, as though they weren't creeping through the biggest storm she'd seen in years.

"Devon Naylor," Callie answered. "You wouldn't know him. I met him in Dallas. He runs a business there."

"You off to live in Dallas then?"

"Yes." Callie was surprised at how forlorn she sounded.

Ross glanced her way with a flash of blue. Ross and his brothers had been the hottest guys in school, but they'd never looked at Callie or her sisters. *Too bad*, she thought wistfully.

"Second thoughts about the big-city life?" Ross asked.

Second, third, and fourth thoughts. "Not used to being closed in," Callie admitted. "Dallas can be fun, but have you seen their traffic? And everyplace you want to go is like a million miles from where you are."

"I hear that. I used to—"

He broke off, his expression changing from lighthearted to grim in a split second. Ross turned his head to stare hard at something on the side of the road, then he abruptly braked.

Callie braced herself as the SUV fishtailed. She held her breath, waiting for another plunge into a ditch, but Ross easily stopped the vehicle, all four tires remaining on the pavement.

He flung open his door, leapt out, and raced away into the silver rain.

Callie craned to keep sight of him as he ran down the road the direction they'd come, the pounding rain misting the pavement. Ross sprinted flat-out, arms and legs pumping, and then he disappeared into the murk.

Shit. Callie tried her phone again, but no, nothing. Stupid

service providers. She should have taken her dad's advice and invested in a sat phone.

A thin young man sprang out of the tall grass behind the SUV and bolted across the road. Callie caught a flash of jeans and a hoodie, and then he was gone.

Ross hurtled out of the grass after him. The chase lasted only a few seconds before Ross, body lithe in his uniform, reached the young man and tackled him.

They went down, but Ross was up in a moment, one hand on the young man's neck. Ross hauled him upright, twisting the kid's arm around his back. The young man fought, but he couldn't break Ross's hold as Ross dragged him to the SUV.

Ross wedged the youth against the side of the vehicle and twisted his other arm behind him, cuffing his wrists in one smooth movement. He opened the back door and shoved the young man inside.

"I wasn't stealing that pickup, Ross," the kid was protesting. "Honest."

"Sure, Manny. That tire iron just happened to leap into your hand."

"It's my truck," Manny said quickly. "I locked my keys inside."

"What's the license plate number?"

"Uh ..."

Ross slammed the door and moved to the front seat.

Manny's hood fell back. Callie saw through the grill that separated back seat from front a freckled face, rain-slicked red hair, gray eyes that probably had the River County girls falling at his feet, and a frank, assessing stare.

"Whoa," Manny said, peering at Callie and her mountain of tulle. "You can get arrested for *that* now?"

Chapter Two

Ross pulled onto the rainy road, trying to keep frustration at bay.

He'd seen Manny out of the corner of his eye, ready to commit grand theft auto on a pickup left on a dirt side road, and Ross wanted to get him before he actually committed it. If Manny had one more conviction on his record, he'd be sent back to the detention center. In four months, he'd be eighteen, and if he broke the law after that, he'd be tried as an adult.

Callie and Manny regarded each other interestedly, Callie unworried that Ross had stopped to pick up a teenage mess. She returned Manny's allover look with an appraising one of her own.

"I'm trying to get married," she answered him. "Unless they've made that a crime. Maybe it should be."

Manny grinned at Ross in the rearview mirror. "You lucky bastard. You should a' told me. I'd have bought you a present."

"I'm not marrying *him*," Callie said with unflattering quickness. "He's giving me a lift."

"He's stupid then," Manny said. "You're gorgeous. Even if you look like a raccoon."

Callie swung around and flipped down the visor, but found no mirror there. She rubbed under her eyes and studied the black that came away on her fingers.

"I guess I do. Crap. There's photographers from every paper in the state waiting for me."

"Really?" Manny asked. "Wow. They'll laugh their asses off."

"Probably," Callie said without rancor.

"Manny," Ross said in warning. Manny leaned forward, intent on him. "Button it," Ross finished curtly.

Manny slammed himself back into his seat. "You are a serious buzz kill, my friend."

"That's my job."

"Yeah? Well, your job sucks."

"Manny." Callie's silken voice slid over teenage anger. "That's an interesting name. Short for Manuel?"

"Manifold Sins," Manny said, the words tight. But amazing, because Manny usually clammed up before he'd reveal his real name. "My mom was a die-hard born-again. Until she died."

"Oh, honey, I'm sorry." Callie said, her sympathy sincere. "It's not a bad thing to have an unusual name, though. Makes you stand out. My sister's called Montana."

"Yeah?" Manny's grin popped back. His moods changed like lightning. "Why?"

"My mom and dad honeymooned there and loved it. So they named their firstborn Montana. No one forgets her name."

"Wish my mom would have loved a place like that. I could be called Wyoming, or something. Or North Carolina."

"When you turn eighteen, you can always change your name," Callie assured him.

"Cool. I could be Dakota Judd."

"Sure, you could," Callie said, grinning back.

Manny switched his attention to Ross. "I really like her,

Ross. You should run away and marry her. She's already got the dress on."

Ross chose not to answer. Bantering with Manny wasn't always wise—the kid could talk rings around the most eloquent lawyers. Sometimes he got sent to juvie just because the judge couldn't figure out what the hell he was going on about.

"Maybe later," Callie said. "Right now I'm marrying someone else. That is, if I can get to the church before everyone leaves."

"Yeah, Ross, why are you going so slow? Lights, sirens, let's go!"

There was no one else on the road in this rain—hail, now. Tiny pellets spattered down, and Ross prayed they stayed tiny. Hail in Texas could become softball-sized in moments, breaking every window in sight.

He felt Callie's imploring gaze. Her lipstick was smudged, like it would be after Ross kissed her.

Shit, why did he think about things like that? His heart started pumping and another part of his anatomy began to respond. *Only natural,* he told himself. *Manny isn't wrong. She's beautiful.*

Callie wasn't marrying just another man, though, but a rich guy from Dallas. Probably a stockbroker or a property developer who rented an entire floor in one of the high-rises downtown, maybe that angled one with the pointed roof. Devon Whoever would stay in his office all day with devoted secretaries who would do *anything* for him, and only occasionally remember he had a beautiful wife at home.

Ross knew he was painting the guy a jerk because he wanted him to be—not good enough for the beautiful woman sitting next to him. Maybe Devon was madly in love with her. He'd buy Callie a present every day, just because, and take long lunches so he could come home and make love to her.

She'd lie beside him in the sunshine, her hair across his pillow, her sleepy blue eyes and wide smile welcoming him.

Ross stiffened. He moved in the seat, willing himself not to have a full-blown hard-on thinking about another guy's soon-to-be wife, with Manny Judd looking over his shoulder.

She was beautiful, but she was taken, and life would go on. Ross would think about her every day of his life, wonder where she was and what she was doing, what would have happened if he'd stuck to his courage and asked her out one day way back when.

His brothers would laugh their asses off if they knew how maudlin he was being.

"You're right, Manny," Ross said, reaching for switches. "Here we go."

The siren sprang to life. Red and blue lights swept through the glittering hail, and Ross stepped on the gas.

The SUV, high-horsepower and in peak condition, sped smoothly down the empty road, fast, faster. Hail sprayed them, the windshield wipers struggling to smack it away.

"Woo hoo!" Callie threw up her hands. "Always wanted to do this."

"Gets old, trust me," Manny said, but he was grinning at Ross, his usually surly face lit up.

Ross kept the accelerator steady, his eye peeled for other cars or animals making a mad dash across the highway. He loved driving fast, but he wasn't stupid.

This road was straight, no curves, as it headed for River-bend. At its end lay the town square with its church, the court-house where Ross worked, and the row of apartments where Ross lived.

The radio clicked. "Ross, what's your twenty?" Mildred asked.

Ross lifted the handheld. "Heading into Riverbend. Five minutes."

"Your mom's worried about you in the hail. And she says the cookout will have to be indoors."

"No kidding. I need to make a drop off at St. Luke's, and then I'm heading in with an arrest. Put new sheets on the cell's bed and flowers on the windowsill."

"Ha ha," Mildred came back. "Did you say St. Luke's?"

"Getting a bride to her groom. Then Manny's coming for a sleepover."

"Manny?" Mildred's voice rose. "What's he done this time?"

"Not my fault, Mrs. Burton," Manny called from the back seat. "Ross is an asshole."

"Watch your mouth, young man," Mildred said sternly. "Ross, Sanchez is heading to town with the tow. Out." She clicked off.

Ahead of them, a hanging light warning of the upcoming stop sign lazily flashed red in the haze.

The hail lightened into heavy rain as Ross pulled to a stop at the intersection. He waited for a lone car to cross slowly in front of him then he drove into the square and around it to St. Luke's.

The small church was a traditional, white-painted, high-steepled building from the very early twentieth century, funded back then by Riverbend's oldest families, which included the Joneses and the Campbells. A colonnaded porch stretched across the front, where on Sundays the congregation jumbled to greet the pastor and make lunch arrangements, and where the Easter egg hunt started every year.

Cars filled the street in front of the church and the tiny parking lot behind. Ross double-parked his patrol SUV next to a bright yellow Ferrari, his lights staining the white church and the people who started filing onto its porch blue and red.

Callie hadn't exaggerated about reporters. Men and women with state-of-the-art digital cameras jostled against the brightly clothed guests, lenses pointed at the SUV.

Ross jumped out and ran around to the passenger side. He knew that people assumed the worst when they saw a law-enforcement vehicle pull up, and he wanted to quickly show them Callie was all right. He yanked open the passenger door and stuck out his hand, ready to help her down as though she were Cinderella descending from her carriage.

"Great," Callie growled under her breath as she scanned the crowded porch. "They're going to love this."

"Give 'em a show," Ross said. He knew as a sheriff's deputy all about how reporters spun stories. "Make them glad they waited."

Callie gave him a nod and a smile, which made the corners of her eyes crinkle.

Damn it, now Ross would start having fantasies about her looking at him like that in the shower. He needed to get her out of here and married off. Felt like a blow to the gut to let her go to someone else, but it was too late, and he had to suck it up.

Callie shoved her skirts out of the door and took firm hold of Ross's arm to climb to the ground. Her satin slipper landed in a puddle, and Callie winced.

But she rallied. She let go of Ross and raised both hands to wave at the waiting crowd.

"You can't say I don't make an entrance," she called.

Catching up her voluminous skirts, she darted around the Ferrari and up the walk to the church.

The reporters *click-clicked* their cameras, but the dozen or so wedding guests and the three bridesmaids in raspberry tulle stood somberly as they watched her come. Something was wrong. They should be waving back, laughing, reaching out to pull Callie excitedly into the church.

Ross remained in the rain, watching her, his heart beating hard in worry. Manny in the back seat pressed his face to the wet window.

Callie ran up the porch steps on light feet. The bridesmaids and a few older women came forward. Ross recognized one of them as Karen Marvin. Figures—Karen liked to be in on any important social event in the county.

Ross couldn't hear what anyone said from the twenty feet of distance between them, but he saw Callie slow, her exuberance fading.

She reached the top step, and the bridesmaids and the woman Ross recognized as Callie's mother converged on her. Callie's arms fell to her sides, limp, and her shoulders sagged.

Ross thought he'd never seen a back so beautiful or so dejected. One wet curl came loose from her bun and dropped to her shoulder.

"Damn." Manny's voice floated to him. "Did he dump her? Or drop dead waiting? Maybe he was an old guy."

Ross didn't bother to tell him to shut up. On the porch, the women surrounded Callie. There was head-shaking, then arms sliding around her. One bridesmaid tried to give her a hug.

Callie broke away from them. Not abruptly, but she pulled back, removing sympathetic hands, before she turned and headed down the steps. They started to follow her, one bridesmaid flinching at the rain before returning to the shelter under the porch roof.

Callie moved slowly but steadily down the walk, looking neither right nor left. One by one, her friends and family dropped back, until Callie walked alone, her skirts dragging on the wet pavement.

She skirted the bright yellow car once more and reached the SUV, where Ross waited by the open door.

Callie looked up at him, her mouth drooping, her eyes filled with a sadness that tore at Ross's heart.

"Deputy Campbell," Callie said quietly. "Will you please drive me home?"

Chapter Three

Ross Campbell was an angel, Callie decided there and then. Not only did he simply bundle her back into the SUV without a word, but he asked no questions, expressed no opinion as he turned off his emergency lights and pulled into the square, taking the road to head out of Riverbend.

Manny, on the other hand, had no such compunctions. "What the hell happened? Is the dude still alive? Or did he get cold feet?"

"Manny," Ross rumbled, but Callie shook her head.

"It's all right. It'll be in all the papers tomorrow. Devon got tired of waiting, and he left, that's all." Heat from rage and humiliation filled her. "I'll call him, and fix it." She glanced at Ross, whose hands remained firmly on the wheel. "You don't really have to drive me all the way home, Ross. I know you have better things to do. Drop me anywhere, and I'll call someone to come get me."

Ross's fleeting blue gaze landed on her. "I'm not leaving you like that in the rain. You still live at your parents' house?"

"Yeah. I do."

Everyone in Riverbend knew which house it was and where it lay. Callie didn't have to bother with directions.

Manny leaned forward. "Aw, that sucks. *He* sucks. Your fiancé, I mean, not Ross. Hey, I know what you should do. Take Ross somewhere and have great revenge sex. You know, serious down-and-dirty—"

"Manny." Ross's neck flushed red, and he clenched the steering wheel.

"I know, I know. Button it." Manny flung himself into the seat, falling silent. Not for long. He started to hum.

Ross said absolutely nothing. Callie raked tears from her face and took a deep breath.

For some reason, deep down, she wasn't surprised that Devon had stormed off. He'd done it before, the last time at a Dallas restaurant when Callie was delayed getting into town. It had taken her days to calm him down from that.

On the church porch, Montana had given Callie a guilt-stricken look and said, "I promise, I thought Evelyn was picking you up. I swear to God."

Evelyn, Callie's second-oldest sister, had cut in. "No, we decided, remember? *You* were supposed to."

Trina, Callie's best friend from Dallas, had hovered behind the sisters. "I'm so sorry, Cal. You know how Devon gets. You should have let me drive you."

Devon's mother had stood a little way from them, a fierce glare on her face. The *That's what my son gets when he tries to marry countrified trash*, kind of look.

Callie's own mother had gazed at her in profound sadness, tears in her eyes. It was her mom's tears, her true sympathy and understanding, that made Callie turn and run. She'd have lost it completely if she'd stayed.

Ross, with her only connection to him their mutual high school and seeing him around town, was neutral and non-judgmental. He'd neither condemn her nor go to pieces.

He did look a little pissed off, probably because of Manny's remarks about revenge sex. Ross breathed fast, and he gripped the steering wheel as though he wanted to arrest it.

But wouldn't it be nice to take Manny's advice? Devon's disapproving face filled her mind, and Callie could hear his voice—*Callie, you know you do this all the time. It's got to stop.*

Right now, she'd love to erase Devon's censure by being alone in a room with Ross, ripping the buttons from his oh-so-pressed uniform shirt, wrapping her arms around him, lifting herself to his firm line of mouth to open it with her tongue …

The vision was so vivid that her temperature spiked. She imagined his smooth shirt, the warmth of the man inside, the incredible strength she'd already experienced when Ross had steadied her. She dug her hands into her ridiculous skirt to keep from reaching for him.

What the hell was wrong with her? She was supposed to be devastated, brokenhearted, bewildered.

Well, bewildered was definitely the case. Why the hell had Devon decided to make a scene on their *wedding day*? She had no doubt he'd been angry—he'd said months ago that her chronic lateness wasn't cute anymore.

The last time had been when the housekeeper's husband collapsed at his office and had to be rushed to the hospital. Callie was happy to drive the distraught woman to be with him, hence her lateness to Dallas and the restaurant. Devon, the pig, had wondered why she'd bothered to help the *help*.

That should have been a clue, Callie knew, though Devon had pretended he was joking at the time.

Why had she thought everything would be all right once she got married? She'd have her own house—*Devon's house*—hang out with Trina, and begin her job at the ranch outside McKinney, where they would rehab rescue horses and either found them new homes or determined that they were too far gone and let them pass peacefully. Callie loved the woman who owned the ranch, and was eager to start, even if Devon's best friend—Trina's husband, Brett—had said *he'd* never want a wife who smelled like horse shit all the time.

The four of them—Trina, Brett, Devon, and Callie—had laughed. Another joke, right?

"What is *wrong* with me?" The words burst out before Callie could stop them. This was *not* the time to have a huge princess rant, but damn, Devon was being a total asshole.

"Nothing wrong with *you*," Ross said with conviction. "Your fiancé's the one who should be twisted into a knot and bounced down the road."

"With his dick cut off," Manny put in with vicious glee.

Callie choked on a laugh and pressed a hand to her mouth. "Quit. I'll start to cry." Tears burned her eyes.

"My advice is, don't call him," Ross said. The drumming of rain on the roof wasn't so loud as the rain slackened once more. "Make him come crawling back to you."

"On his ass," Manny added.

"What I mean is," Ross cut through Manny's words. "You have nothing to apologize for. *He* does. You were late, through no fault of your own. He got impatient and deserted you—at your wedding. Huge difference. He's the one who should beg for forgiveness."

His tone was harsh, and Callie looked at him in surprise. "You sound like this has happened before." To him, maybe?

Ross shook his head. "Not this exact thing, but I've seen a lot of people get into it. As soon as you make another person's behavior your fault, they have their fist around you. Pretty soon you're taking the blame for every little thing, and that can escalate into a bad situation very fast."

"He knows what he's talking about," Manny said. "Happened to my mom and dad, except my dad was the one under my mom's thumb. Now he's just a useless drunk."

Callie's anger eased as she softened in compassion for Manny. Being left at the altar was shitty and humiliating, and she'd hear about it the rest of her life in this small town, but at least she had a loving family in which to recover. She'd not grown up with the grimness she saw in Manny's and Ross's faces.

"Don't worry," she said, directing her words to both of them. "I won't call Devon."

Callie suddenly never wanted to speak to the man again. She'd thought it would be so much fun to marry the best friend of her best friend's husband. They were inseparable, a team. At first, it had been wonderful. Her sisters loved Trina but didn't intrude on the friendship. They'd liked Brett and Devon. Trina had been thrilled when Devon had asked Callie to marry him.

Then slowly, gradually, both Devon and Brett had started turning into dickheads. Maybe they always had been, and Callie had been too busy with her Dallas job and planning the ranch to notice.

They passed the stretch of road where Callie's tire had decided to blow, and she'd ended up in the ditch. The Mercedes was gone, but the troughs in the grass she'd plowed up remained.

"K.D. picked up your car," Ross said. "He's the best mechanic in the county. Has his shop on the Fredericksburg highway."

"Yeah, I've seen it."

Callie couldn't worry about her car right now—that would come later. Right now, she needed to get home. She'd take a calming shower and then head out to the barn where her real friends were. She always felt better around horses. *They* didn't care who she married or whether she'd been left in the rain, embarrassed in front of everyone she'd grown up with plus strangers from Dallas with spite in their eyes.

After another rainy five miles, Ross slowed unerringly at the arched gateway that led to the Jones ranch. He turned without sliding on the wet pavement and navigated the mile-long muddy drive with ease.

"Holy shit!" Manny said in awe as the house came into view. "You live *here*?"

The white monolith of Callie's family home rose from a vast green lawn, the house's many windows and black shutters a popular design when it had been built in 1845. The drive curved to the front door, running under a two-story portico supported by massive columns. A huge black square lantern that hung from a long chain in the center of the portico had lit the way into the house for generations. In the past, candle flame had welcomed guests; now it was LEDs.

"It's like the house in that movie," Manny breathed. "What's it called? *Gone with the Wind*."

"Same era," Callie said. "Pre Civil War."

"I think my dad's trailer was built back then too," Manny said.

His joke evoked Callie's sympathy once more. "Then you'll know that living in a two-hundred year old house isn't as romantic as it sounds. We're always fixing something."

"Yeah, so are we."

Ross pulled smoothly to a halt under the portico, the drive empty of cars, as everyone thankfully was still in town. Ross shot a warning look at Manny before he got out, strode around to Callie's side, and as he had at the church, gallantly opened the door for her.

The touch of his hand as he helped her out had Callie drawing a quick breath before the caring look in his eyes made that breath vanish.

Callie jerked her hand away as though it burned and hurried to the front door. Her keys were now either in K.D.'s auto shop or with the deputy Ross had called, but that was no worry. She shoved her skirts out of the way, moved the rock behind the bench on the porch, and pulled out a key.

"That's dangerous," Ross admonished.

"But seriously handy." Callie put the key into the lock and turned it, hearing the click echo through the empty house.

"Hide it somewhere else from now on. Manny saw you."

Callie glanced at Ross in surprise then at the SUV from which Manny watched avidly. "You think he'd rob us? He doesn't look much like a criminal."

"He was my first arrest," Ross said as Callie pushed open the front door to reveal a grand foyer with a black-and-white tiled floor and a staircase that rose gracefully to the upper stories. "Manny was ten, but that wasn't our last rodeo. He's not a bad kid—he just gets in with the wrong people, and they offer him money to steal cars, break into places, whatever. Manny needs the money because his dad hasn't held onto a job in years—he wasn't lying when he said his dad was always drunk. Whenever child protection services come sniffing around, his dad cleans up his act and plays the part of the worried but virtuous father until they go away again. Manny doesn't want to leave his dad—he loves him and thinks he's taking care of him."

Callie leaned against the doorframe, her skirt filling up most of the space, the tulle pressing Ross's legs.

"Are you really going to take him to jail?" she asked. Talking about Manny was a hell of a lot safer than talking about herself.

"No." Ross let out a breath. "I'll let him go, but I'll keep an eye on him. I need him to shape up, though, and soon, or it will be too late for me to help him."

Callie couldn't stop her smile. "You're a good person, Ross Campbell."

"That's what people think, anyway." He paused. "Callie."

She'd started to turn away, but when Ross said her name in his deep voice, she quickly turned back.

He hadn't moved, or reached for her, but he pinned her in place with only a look. "If you need to talk, call me. I mean it." Ross took a card from the heavy belt that housed his gun and cuffs and held it out to her between blunt fingers.

She saw his name and title in tasteful brown-gold print,

along with the logo of the River County Sheriff's Department. The phone number on it couldn't be his personal one, Callie reasoned as she took it. He meant she should call him at his office.

Callie slid her thumb across the card, liking the bumps of his embossed name. "Are you saying a guy wants to listen to a girl whine about her problems?"

Ross's grin returned, the one that warmed like a thousand suns. "I have four sisters-in-law, a niece, and a mom. I'm used to it." His smile died. "Seriously. What you're going through isn't something you can shrug off. And sometimes family is too close."

He wrapped his hand around hers, closing her fingers over the card.

Callie's throat went dry, and her chest constricted. She tried to draw a breath, but her lungs no longer worked.

Ross's hand was hot, callused, strong. The touch of it ignited feelings it had no business igniting. Callie's vivid imagination called up sensations of Ross's touch on her body, his hard palm on her breast then a slow glide down her belly, moving further to cup between her thighs.

Callie gulped, and air sailed into her to make her dizzy. The doorframe, thank heavens, held her up, or her melting knees would have dropped her to the floor.

Reaction. Must be. She was upset about Devon and the wedding—her entire life—and Ross was standing close, warming her. Her knight in shining armor, the one who'd saved her from hell and brought her to safety. Normal to want to jump his bones, she reasoned.

But Ross was simply being nice, helping out an old acquaintance. They'd grown up in the same town, shared a bond.

Ross would go back to work, Callie would fix this disaster, and she wouldn't see Ross again. Maybe in passing when she went into Riverbend, but nothing more.

Mostly, Callie planned to stay home and grow old until everyone forgot about her and her humiliating almost-wedding.

She needed wine.

She jerked her hand from Ross's, and he released her without a word. He'd meant nothing by his touch. A friendly gesture, that was all.

"Thanks, Ross," Callie said hurriedly. "I'll see you."

Somehow, she got her skirts inside the door. She looked forward to ripping the wet tulle apart and stuffing it into the trash, along with the ruined silk bodice.

"See you, Callie." His handsome Campbell face and easy stance made her want to grab his hand, drag him inside, and not let him go.

But she'd imposed on him enough, he had Manny to see to, and a family dinner to attend.

She drew breath and forced herself to swing the heavy door shut. Ross moved out of its way, not worried when it slammed more or less in his face.

Callie watched through the door's sidelight as Ross strode back to the SUV, his uniform hugging a very nice ass. He said something to Manny in the back, then unhurriedly slid into the driver's seat and closed the door.

In another moment, he drove away, leaving Callie's life as easily as he'd entered it.

Callie slid out of her satin shoes and swept them into her hand. She took two steps up the staircase, then collapsed onto it, cradling her head on her arms and weeping without remorse.

ON A SWELTERING MID-JULY DAY WITH TEMPS IN THE hundreds, Mildred called across the sheriff's office.

"Ross! Callie Jones is on the line for you."

All desks were empty except for Mildred's, Ross's, and Rafe Sanchez's. Sanchez looked up with eager interest.

"Hey, wish a rain-drenched, rich bride would call *me*."

Mildred answered him. "If you took one home after she was left at the altar, maybe one would. Ross?"

Ross prayed Mildred had put Callie on hold, and Callie hadn't heard the exchange.

He'd been waiting for this call for months. Didn't realize how much until right now. His mouth went dry, and his head buzzed like he'd contracted a sudden fever.

"Forward it to my cell," he said as calmly as he could.

"Personal calls at the office." Sanchez shook his head and went back to his computer. "Hennessey isn't going to like that."

"It's not personal," Mildred said. "She called the main line. Ross? You ready?"

Ross shoved himself from his desk, snatching up his cell phone. "Ready." He gave Sanchez, his grinning best friend, the finger, and walked out into the courthouse hall.

He tapped his phone after it got in one peep of a ring and lifted it to his ear. "Callie? You okay?"

"Hi, Ross." She sounded perfectly fine. Sweet Texas drawl, her voice like satin. Fine, but a little worried.

"What's wrong?" Ross heard his tone go sharp. He couldn't remain neutral and businesslike around this woman.

"It's Manny," Callie said. "I wasn't sure who to call."

"Is he hurt?" he asked, fear stabbing him surprisingly hard.

"No, nothing like that. But ..."

Ross let out a breath, leaned against a cool wall, and pinched the bridge of his nose. "Son of a ... Where is he? What did he do?"

"Well ..." Callie hesitated, and he imagined her gazing into space as she thought. She'd be wearing ... what? Ross couldn't stop picturing her in her sopping wedding gown, the white silk hugging her curves, the glitter dusting her skin. Wet, beautiful woman.

"He's here — at our house. He broke into one of the sheds."

"Shit," Ross said in dismay. Three more weeks and Manny was eighteen. "What did he take?" *Please, let it be nothing worth more than twenty bucks.*

"The tractor mower," Callie said, a strange note in her voice.

"*Damn* it. Sit tight — he can't go far with something like that. I'll get it back in one piece and talk — "

"No, no, he didn't steal it," Callie cut him off. "He's mowing the lawn with it. I'm calling you because we can't make him stop."

Chapter Four

✦✦✦

Callie paced the front veranda until dust on the drive announced the arrival of a sheriff's SUV. She strained to see who was driving, but the sun glinting on the windshield blocked her view.

After his startled, "What the hell?" Ross had quickly said that someone would be right over. Hadn't said it would be him.

Callie hated that she'd dashed to her bathroom and made sure her hair was combed, but didn't *look* like she'd run to comb it. Casually neat, as though she'd just returned from riding. But not what she really looked like when she came in from the stables, which was sweat-streaked face and hat hair.

She checked her clothes—jeans, colorful top with three-quarter sleeves, jodhpur boots. Just another ranch girl. With makeup and a little lip gloss. Sure.

The SUV halted a few feet beyond the portico, remaining in the sun. No lights or sirens. Callie saw the shape of a man beyond the tinted windows, but which man, she couldn't tell.

He took his time, tapping at his computer and talking into his radio, while Callie stood in agony. Should she run out to the SUV to greet him? Or stand here like a poised young lady who'd been a debutante, cotillion and all?

The SUV door opened. Callie let out her held breath in a rush when she saw Ross with his dark hair and tight body, the uniform emphasizing his trim build.

"Where is he?" Ross asked her.

No, *Hey, Callie. How you doing? You been holding up all right?* He was tense, angry, ready to grab Manny and haul him away.

"Around back." Callie waved Ross to follow her along the narrow gravel path that led behind the house.

The manor was surrounded by an expanse of lawn that swept in a swath of green down to the stables, horse corrals, and a small covered riding ring. The tended lawn blended into the Texas grasslands about there, with Hill Country scrub, trees, and rolling hills taking over. The heart of the ranch was wild country where the cattle roamed and Callie liked to ride, leaving her troubles behind.

The bright green lawn, kept in pristine condition by a team of gardeners, was a beautiful place to walk, and where Callie's mother hosted her popular parties.

Halfway down the hill, a small red tractor cut a sharp turn across the grass, leaving a jagged stripe in his wake.

"He's been at it almost an hour," Callie said. "My dad is going to shit when he sees what's happened to his lawn."

"Hell. Callie, I'm sorry."

Ross scowled at the tractor in the distance, his jaw clenched. Sunglasses hid his eyes, but Callie decided that Ross in the sunshine looked even better than Ross in the rain.

She swallowed the lump in her throat. "Why should you be sorry? Unless you sent him ...?"

She was joking, but Ross slanted her a sharp look. "Sent him? What would I do that for?"

"To give you an excuse to come over and ask me out?"

What the hell had made her say that? Callie clamped her

mouth shut, her heart jumping all over the place. A bead of sweat ran from her temple to tickle her ear.

Ross stared at her from behind his sunglasses, not moving a muscle. Callie made herself gaze back at him, her smile fixed. She must look like a weird, grinning plastic clown.

Manny yelled. The tractor took another abrupt turn then kept going in a circle, Manny struggling with the controls.

Ross took off across the grass. Callie, after a startled second, ran behind him. Ross, with his long stride, quickly reached the tractor. He leapt onto the step beside the seat, gloved hand reaching down to turn off the machine.

The tractor coasted to a halt. Ross pulled up the cutting blade and set the brake.

Callie reached them, her boots pinching her feet—they were made for riding not running—her breath coming in gasps.

"Manny, what on earth are you doing?" was all she could get out.

"Mowing the lawn." Manny flashed her a grin as he climbed stiffly off the tractor. His legs buckled, but Ross caught him and shoved him upright.

Manny was nearly as tall as Ross, the seventeen-year-old already filling out into the man he'd become. His red hair gleamed in the sunshine, and his cocky smile lit up his eyes. Yep, Callie bet he was a heartbreaker.

Like Ross had been. Callie remembered the long-ago, sunny October high school day when Ross had approached her. She'd been standing outside at lunch, her friends having gone en masse to the bathroom, but she'd wanted to drink in more of the outdoors before being cooped up the rest of the day.

Ross Campbell had walked toward her with his lanky saunter, jeans outlining strong legs. A T-shirt had stretched across a hard body, and the brim of his cowboy hat shaded his tanned face. She'd noticed him looking at her for the few weeks prior to this, ever since she'd encountered him at his locker and he'd drawled a charming politeness. He'd glanced at Callie whenever they'd passed, as though he might want to speak to her but hadn't made up his mind.

Callie had wet her lips as he'd approached, trying to stay cool, trying to pretend only mild interest. She was so sure he'd to ask her to the homecoming dance—had hoped with all her heart.

When he'd only winked at her as he'd leaned against the fence and asked her what he'd missed in their Spanish class last week, her disappointment had been fierce.

She'd thought the great-looking Ross had liked her, but he'd only wanted the smart girl's notes. The rawness of that had followed her for a long time, but she hadn't blamed Ross. Stupid Callie for thinking he had any interest in her.

Callie snapped herself back to the present, and a grinning Manny. "*Why* were you mowing the lawn?" she asked him.

Manny shrugged. "Ross told me I should get a job, you know, a real one. You have a big yard. I thought I'd help out."

Ross made a noise of exasperation. "Most people knock on the door and *ask* first."

"Yeah? What if they say *Get lost, you waste of space*? This way, I've already done the work, and they have to pay me."

"This is *not* what I was talking about," Ross growled.

"Don't worry about it," Callie said quickly. "He didn't hurt anything. Well …" She gazed at the third of the lawn with crazy, uneven stripes. "Nothing that can't be fixed. It's only grass."

"Not the point," Ross said. "Of all the dumbass things you've done … This has to be the weirdest."

"No, it's not. You came over, didn't you? Did you ask her out yet?"

Callie's face burned at the same time Ross flushed.

Manny looked back and forth between them. "Oh, you *did* ask her. What, you said no?" he said to Callie, surprised.

"*I* asked *him*." The searing heat in Callie's cheeks trickled to her neck and chest. "Sort of. He hasn't answered yet."

"Yeah? So, what's wrong with you, Ross? If a lady like her asked *me* out, I'd already be in the truck with her and halfway down the road."

Ross laid a hand on Manny's shoulder. "This is none of your business, son. We're going to the station to have a talk."

"No." At Callie's impassioned word, both men turned to her. Now the heat ran all the way to her toes. "He didn't do anything wrong."

Ross's mouth firmed. "Trespassing, breaking and entering, property damage."

"I don't want to bring any charges," Callie said. "Give him a break, Ross."

"Yeah, Ross, give me a break."

Ross released Manny and removed his sunglasses. White lines creased the tan at his temples, and his eyes glittered.

"All right," he said to Manny, "but you're going to fix anything you've broken, and you're going to mow the rest of this lawn, but the right way."

"Sorry." Manny scuffed the ground with his toe, embarrassed. "I've never driven a tractor mower—I've never had a lawn this big. Hell, we don't even have a lawn. Just dirt where I live."

Ross shot Callie a look, then slid his sunglasses back on. "It's not hard. Here, I'll show you."

Callie hid a smile as Ross led Manny to the mower and began pointing out the levers. Manny swung into the driver's seat, and Ross stood on the running board, holding on to the seat as Manny started up and moved off.

She watched them for a while, Manny driving slowly, Ross patiently showing him how to mow a straight row.

They'd be hot and thirsty when they were done. Callie ducked into the house and the kitchen, which looked out over the back. Ross and Manny rode up and down the lawn while

Callie brewed up a batch of tea and poured it into a pitcher with ice.

She felt like her mom carrying a tray with the pitcher and glasses to the back veranda, setting it up on the table. But why not? Her mom had always done thoughtful things for them. Everyone knew Caitlyn Jones loved her family and her husband. Even now, Callie's parents had taken a vacation, just the two of them, to South Padre Island to enjoy a B&B and the beach.

They'd been reluctant to leave Callie alone, but Callie had pushed them out the door. She wasn't a baby anymore, and she welcomed the time by herself to heal.

Ross and Manny at last parked the tractor. The lawn looked better, Manny's squiggles smoothed into more or less straight lines.

Both men leapt lightly up the steps to the veranda, the younger and the older. *What Ross had been and what he'd become*, Callie thought.

"I made y'all iced tea," she said brightly. "Manny, you want sugar? We don't do sweet tea at my house—we fix it up as we like it." She indicated the sugar bowl and spoon on the tray.

"Cool." Manny snatched the cover off the sugar bowl, staining the porcelain with grass and dirt. She'd be washing that before her mom came home.

Manny shoveled five tablespoons of sugar into his tea and stirred vigorously. Ross used his own spoon and took a scoop. Callie drank hers unsweetened.

"You live the life." Manny sat back in the rocking chair, stretched out his long legs, and sipped his tea. He gazed over the grass to the stables and let out an "Ah…"

Ross rolled his eyes.

"Well?" Callie asked Ross, pretending her hands weren't shaking. "Are you going to ask me out? After Manny's gone to all this trouble?"

Manny lifted his head, blatantly listening. Callie's heart beat faster, her fingers twitching on her cold glass.

"Sure," Ross said. "Callie, you want to grab some coffee at the diner when I'm off shift?"

Manny banged his head into the back of the wooden rocker. "Real smooth, dude. A woman like Callie wants to go to a fancy restaurant. Not Mrs. Ward's in Riverbend."

"Coffee at the diner sounds great," Callie said in her best polite voice.

"Good," Ross said. "I'm done at six. Meet you there around six-thirty?"

"Sure."

They were both brittle, overly friendly, tense.

Manny groaned. "I give up on you, man."

Callie jumped to her feet. "Manny, can you help me carry the dishes back inside?"

Ross was up before she was standing. He reached for the tray. "I got this."

His hands bumped Callie's, like in a bad romantic comedy. The burn of his touch startled her, and she jerked away. Fortunately, Ross had a good hold of the tray and lifted it with ease.

They went into the house, Ross leading with the tray and pitcher, Callie following with glasses and napkins, Manny shuffling behind them with his own empty glass.

"Wow," Manny said as they entered through the French door. "This kitchen is bigger than my whole house." He gazed at the spread of cabinets, black counters, giant refrigerator, and work island that separated the kitchen from the living room. About fifteen years ago, Callie's parents had decided to take out walls and open up space, so the right half of the house was one huge room.

Ross said nothing, only put the dishes in the sink. He came from an old ranching family, as Callie did, and probably wasn't impressed with big living spaces.

She'd seen his house up close only once, when she'd gone

with a charity group to take kids to meet horses. Ross's mom opened the ranch to disadvantaged children, and Callie's debutante group had escorted them to Circle C Ranch. The boys and girls had met horses and ridden gentle ones and talked to the Campbell brothers, who'd demonstrated their trick riding.

The Campbell home was a traditional ranch house, one-story and rambling, added onto whenever necessary. It had a big, wraparound porch with a jumble of chairs, porch swings, and tables so the brothers could collapse whenever they wanted. It was a friendly, informal, inviting place.

Callie loved her family's house, where she'd grown up with her sisters, but these days it was too quiet. She could hear the big clock ticking on the landing in the staircase hall, the creak of water in the pipes, the rustle of birds nesting in the ivy.

The house had been full of noise when she'd been younger —she and her sisters had *not* been sweet, well-behaved angels —but now that Montana and Evelyn had their own places— both in Austin—and their parents traveled so much, the house was silent. While the quiet of the last few months had been what Callie needed, Manny's exuberance was a welcome change.

Ross ran tap water, rinsing out the glasses, while Manny wandered around the large kitchen and into the living room.

"Damn," he said softly as he turned slowly in place. "I get to tell all my dudes I was in the Jones's house."

Ross snapped off the water and grabbed a towel to wipe his hands. "I don't want any of those dudes coming here, understand me?"

Manny glanced at him in surprise. "No way. They got no class at all. Callie invited *me* in, not them."

"Which was real nice of her," Ross said. "Now I'm taking you home."

Manny sent Callie an appealing look. "Day's young. I can mow the rest of the yard."

Callie read behind his eyes that he'd rather do anything,

anything, even be locked in a jail cell, than go home. She'd asked around about Manny since her disastrous, almost wedding day, and heard sad answers.

"That would be fine with me," Callie said. "How about it, Ross? He knows what he's doing now. You mow, Manny, and I'll pay you—fifty dollars?"

Ross started to rumble something, but Manny punched the air. "Yes!" He ran out the back door, slamming it until the glass rattled, and sprinted for the mower.

"Are you sure?" Ross asked Callie. "I can't stay and watch him ..."

"He'll be fine," Callie said, believing it. "He just wants to help."

"I know. He runs with bad guys. They give him a couple hundred dollars to do errands for them, or be a lookout, or whatever. It's a hell of a lot more than he'd make at minimum wage—if anyone would even hire him—and he knows it."

"Well, this is an honest job and I'll give him honest pay," Callie said. "He's got to start somewhere."

Ross slid on his sunglasses. They hid his sexy eyes but at the same time gave him a new dimension of hot.

"If he does anything besides mow the lawn, call me. I like the kid, but don't make the mistake of trusting him too much. Manny doesn't understand the difference between right and wrong—or maybe he knows, but he doesn't understand why he needs to follow it."

Callie watched Manny hunker over the tractor's wheel, determined to keep it on the straight path. "I heard that after his mom died, his dad withdrew into himself and didn't come out," she said. "He's had to raise himself."

"Making him a target for every criminal in the area who needs cheap labor."

Callie blinked. "Are there that many criminals in River County?" She scanned the horizon, green hills as far as she could see. "Where are they hiding?"

"You don't want to know." Ross's brows appeared briefly over his sunglasses and went down again. "You really don't."

The peace of the day was broken only by Manny's shout of triumph when he successfully negotiated a turn at the end of a row. Down near the stables, the men and women hired to clean stalls and feed the horses were lazing in the shade, taking a break.

The setting was tranquil, and Callie had always felt safe here. It was sanctuary. But Ross must know where the hidden meth houses were, where the enclaves of crime were tucked even in the most picturesque of towns in this county. She suppressed a shiver.

"Call me if he screws up," Ross said. "See you at six-thirty?"

"We don't have to go," Callie said quickly. "I mean, if you asked me to make Manny be quiet, that's fine. I'm sure you have a life to get back to."

Ross looked at her a long time, but she couldn't read the thoughts behind his sunglasses. "See you at six-thirty," he said firmly. "If you change your mind and don't want to come, okay. But I'll be there for my coffee."

Callie swallowed. "Well, all right." She tried to sound indifferent, tried to give him a little smile. She hoped he couldn't see her lips shake. "See you then."

Ross gazed at her a while longer before he gave her a minute nod, turned, and walked around the house to his SUV. His black utility belt made his backside sway a bit, which was no bad thing.

Callie found her tongue stuck to the roof of her mouth as she followed at a polite distance, her eyes dry from staring. Ross climbed into his SUV and reached for his radio, and still she stared, though she could barely see him through the glass.

He started the SUV and slowly pulled off. Callie waved then forced her arm down before she kept on waving like an idiot.

Six-thirty. Four hours away. Not even close to enough time to get ready.

SHE WASN'T COMING. ROSS CLICKED HIS EMPTY COFFEE CUP to the table and waved off the waitress who immediately arrived to top it off.

When Callie had told him they didn't have to keep the date, he should have realized she was trying to let him down easy. She'd only agreed because she'd seen through Manny's transparent ploy to fix them up, and she hadn't wanted to hurt the kid's feelings.

Wishful thinking, Ross told himself. He'd changed out of his uniform at home, dashing around like a fool trying to find something decent to wear. He'd settled on jeans and a black button-down shirt, cowboy boots as usual.

It was seven-thirty by the regulator clock on the wall, which tick-tick-ticked away the minutes. Callie wasn't coming.

"How's it going, Ross?"

The seat across the table filled with the bulk of Kyle Malory.

The Malorys were longtime rivals of the Campbell brothers, though lately they'd become tolerable friends and, in a roundabout way, in-laws. Kyle's sister Grace had married Ross's brother Carter. Carter was adopted, so not a blood brother of the Campbells, but he was legally in their family, and accepted by the rest of the Campbells as one of them. Meant Ross and Kyle were sort-of brothers by marriage now.

"It's going," Ross said. "You?"

"I heard you ran out to the Jones ranch and stayed a while," Kyle said. "To see Callie? Who made a run for your sheriff's car on her wedding day?"

A scowl pulled at Ross's mouth. "I swear you have better things to talk about than Callie and her problems."

"Her neighbors don't," Kyle returned, undeterred. "Heard you were there for an hour or so. What happened? She report a break-in?"

"Sort of." Ross didn't elaborate. None of Kyle's business. A cop didn't give out a litany of what calls he'd answered all day, especially not in a town as gossipy as this one.

Kyle lifted his hands. "Hey, I'm just repeating what I heard. Making sure everything's fine at the Jones's."

"Sure, you are. Here's a tip, Kyle. Don't listen to nosy neighbors."

Kyle chuckled. "There's no other kind in Riverbend. Your mom still doing her summer barbecue next week?"

"Haven't heard her calling it off. Why would she?"

"In case Jess has her kid? Last time I saw Jess, she looked ready to pop. Your brothers keep pushing out the babies."

Jess, Tyler's wife, was due any second, but nothing stopped the Campbell traditions.

"You know my mom will have her barbecue and deliver the baby personally at the same time," Ross said. "Plus run all the ranch business from her phone."

Kyle conceded with a nod. "Yeah, your mom's something."

The Campbell's mother, Olivia, after her husband passed, had raised four boys and run Circle C ranch on her own, adding Carter to the mix when Ross had been ten. Olivia had never married again, had never dated seriously, though Ross had always put that down to her being perpetually busy and still grieving their dad.

But the Campbell boys had now become men, four of the five were married, and maybe it was time Olivia saw to her own happiness.

"Hey." A breathless, female, and very sexy voice sounded somewhere to his right. "Sorry I'm late."

Callie. She was here.

Chapter Five

Callie smiled down at him, and Ross came instantly to his feet.

Why had God made her so beautiful? Stupid people called her the least attractive of the sisters, and Ross couldn't figure out why.

Maybe her not-quite-straight nose. Or her hair that was a mixture of brown and blond, like it couldn't decide. Her smile that was too wide for her face. Or the way her eyes flashed when she spoke. Or maybe those people were just looking at her and not listening to the soft note in her voice, the tone that made dark things in him stir.

"Ross?" Callie waved her hand in front of his face. "I really am sorry. One of the mares got sick, and I wanted to wait for the vet. She's okay—the mare, I mean, not the vet. Though Anna seemed okay too." Callie's smile spread. Anna Lawler, the large-animal vet, was a petite young woman and didn't care who thought her job too rough for her.

Ross cleared his throat. He sensed Kyle, who'd risen behind him, grinning like a shithead.

"No problem," Ross managed. "Sit down. I'll get you some coffee."

He signaled the waitress so abruptly he almost smacked Kyle in the face. Kyle sidestepped, his amusement not dimming.

"Hey, Callie," Kyle said. "How's your folks?"

Callie turned her politeness on him. "Oh fine, last time they checked in. They're having a romantic getaway." Her nose wrinkled. "They're so sweet."

Happy parents. Ross was glad she had that.

Kyle swept out a chair for Callie before Ross could. Ross decided not to deck him—or arrest him—and waited for Callie to sit. She gave Kyle a gracious nod, and again Ross held himself back from punching the man.

"Good to see you, Kyle." Ross gave him a pointed look.

Kyle was loving this. He remained next to the table a little longer, just to be a dickhead. "See you round, Callie. Maybe talk to you at the Campbell barbecue?"

Olivia invited the whole town to her annual do, which raised money for the homes for troubled boys she supported. Callie hesitated.

"Oh, I don't know if—"

"My mom would love it if you came," Ross said, not exaggerating. Olivia was thrilled whenever a Jones turned up at her barbecue—they drew a lot of attention and their presence encouraged others to attend. "She'll waive the ticket cost."

"No, she doesn't have to do that ..."

"She'll do it whether you like it or not, knowing her," Ross said.

"Well, I'll see if I can. Thanks." Callie's cheeks were pink, her discomfort obvious.

Ross scowled at Kyle. "Pretty sure there's someplace you need to be."

Kyle ignored him. "I used to pick on Ross something bad when he was a kid. Then his brothers would haul me off him and beat on me, and Ray would jump into the fray to defend *me*. Ross would get up, brush himself off, and watch us pummel each other. Now that he's all growed up, with a badge and gun, he won't let us get away with shit."

Ross folded his arms. "That's right. Say hi to Ray for me."

"You bet. Give my best to your mama and all your sisters-in-law. There's hell of a lot of Campbells now."

"One of them's your sister," Ross reminded him. "Take care, bro."

Kyle's face darkened the slightest bit, then his smile flashed out once more. Kyle had been less than thrilled when Grace had announced she'd marry Carter, but he'd come around, especially after their first baby had been born. Now he was a devoted uncle.

Finally, after another million years, Kyle said good-bye and sauntered off, taking his cowboy hat from the stand at the door before he departed.

"Malorys." Ross sat down as the waitress, looking amused, set an empty cup in front of Callie, then filled both cups with hot brew. "Want any pie, Callie?" Ross asked. "Pecan is the specialty today."

He regretted the words as soon as he said them—some women grew offended if offered food that might put an ounce on their hips. He'd once gone out with a woman who'd refused to eat anything but a few leaves of lettuce.

"I love pecan pie," Callie gushed. "Sounds like the perfect end to my day. Put lots of whipped cream on it," she told the waitress, who was one of Mrs. Ward's daughters.

"You got it." She made a note on her pad. "Two slices of pecan pie. One with extra whipped cream."

The waitress scooted off, a bounce in her step. Everyone was laughing at Ross tonight.

"Hope your horse is all right," Ross said. At least ranchers could talk about animals if they couldn't think of anything else to say.

"Oh, yeah, she is. It was gas." Callie toyed with the napkin holder as she spoke. "She got a belly full of it and was groaning and rolling around. We were worried, but Anna had her up and fine in no time. I didn't mean to keep you waiting, but I didn't want to run off until I knew she was okay. I would have called but I didn't want to phone your office again."

"Hey, you don't have to apologize."

Callie looked up at him, and Ross was stunned to see stark fear in her eyes. Afraid of Ross's reaction to her tardiness? Or something else?

He covered her hand with his.

Callie's eyes widened, and she glanced at the filled tables around them. Everyone would have caught Ross's move, and it would be all over town tomorrow.

Ross didn't lift his hand. Callie's fingers were cold under his, but also soft, smooth, lovely.

"What's wrong?" he asked. "It's just coffee and pie. Not the apocalypse."

Callie didn't jerk away, but she didn't relax. "If you want the truth, I seriously debated coming this evening. I haven't gone out much, you know, since ..."

Since her asshole of a fiancé had humiliated her in front of the entire town.

"This isn't *out*," Ross said. Even Manny had recognized the difference. "This is Mrs. Ward's diner. It's like most people's living rooms. My sister-in-law is in the kitchen even now, whipping up pastries for tomorrow's breakfast crowd."

Callie sent him a fleeting smile. "Thanks for trying to make me feel better. It's been tough."

Ross gently moved his hand. "If you're worried about people talking about you—first, everyone in Riverbend talks about everybody else, and second, what happened was *his* fault, not yours. He's the outsider, and he hurt one of our own. The town's on your side, Callie."

She flushed. "Maybe—that's real sweet—but still. It's

embarrassing. Everyone feels sorry for me, and I'll never be able to shake that. I'm always going to be the Jones girl who got left at the altar."

She was right, and Ross couldn't deny it. Even Kyle had described her so — *Callie? Who made a run for your sheriff's car on her wedding day?*

The wedding guests had witnessed Ross drive Callie to the church and Ross drive her home. The only reason *that* gossip hadn't stirred into a wildfire was because they'd seen Manny with them, and Ross returning not long later to drive Manny to the trailer park on the west side of town. Plus he'd turned up at Circle C after that to cook dinner.

Now Callie was meeting Ross for coffee, and everyone in the diner watched, waiting to go home and talk about it.

Mrs. Ward's daughter breezed back with two giant slices of pie, one piled so high with whipped cream that no pie could be seen beneath it. She sloshed more coffee into the cups they'd barely touched. "Enjoy," she said brightly, and rushed away again.

"Maybe I should ask for a box," Callie said, eyeing her slice. "I'll eat it at home."

Ross looked around the diner. Yep, everyone was interested. Most pretended not to be, but some blatantly stared. There was Jack Hillman, one of Carter's friends, more biker than cowboy. Jack had curiosity on his bearded face, his tattooed hands lifting a giant burger as he eyed them. Mr. Carew, the sleekly dressed head of the bank, ate quietly by himself but kept his attention on Ross and Callie in the corner.

At least none of Ross's brothers were here at the moment. He could be thankful for that.

"Fuck 'em," Ross said.

Callie jumped. "Beg your pardon?"

"Fuck 'em." He lifted his fork. "Eat your pie. Live your life. To hell with them."

"Oh." Callie slid her fork from the paper napkin rolled around it. "I see what you mean."

She dug into the mountain of cream and shoved a huge forkful into her mouth.

There was so much cream it slathered across her lips and dropped to her chin. Callie burst into laughter, grabbed her napkin, and pressed it to her face.

Ross watched her eyes light up, making her even more beautiful. She moved her napkin to reveal the cream smeared all over her lips. Ross wanted to lean over and lick it off, and the need shot through his veins.

"I think it went up my nose." Callie's eyes sparkled with merriment.

"Well, that's a hell of a lot of whipped cream. Let me help you with that." Ross scooped up a gob from her plate, making sure his hand didn't shake, and ate it himself. "Mmm. Damn good. I like how Mrs. Ward puts cinnamon in it."

Callie nodded, her napkin again on her mouth. "It's great."

"Better eat it up then. Before I do."

She wiped her face and lowered her napkin, her lips flecked with cream. Ross stopped his finger from floating forward and brushing the dots from her mouth. He'd revel in the soft warmth of her lips, but then the town's cellular system might crash with all the texting he'd cause.

Callie stabbed at the pie, pushing aside the whipped cream, and ate a bite. "This really is good."

"Mrs. Ward makes one hell of a pie."

"I know. I don't have the chance to try it very often."

"Poor little rich girl." Ross gave her sad eyes. "You had to have your personal cook make you pie."

As he'd hoped, he made Callie's worry flee. She gave him a mock severe look and pointed her fork at him. "See, that's the kind of attitude that drives me nuts. My mom cooked all our meals, and taught us how too—she only has help for her parties, like your mom. My folks didn't hand my sisters and me everything because we asked for it, and they still don't. We went to college on academic scholarships, and we work at real jobs ..." She trailed off. "At least I was."

"Yeah? What were you doing?"

Ross had teased her to animate her. The Jones sisters had always been proud they could stand on their own feet, and the moroseness in Callie's voice tugged him.

"I was going to work at a rehab ranch in Dallas," she said. "Rescuing horses from bad situations, or ones coming off the tracks or rodeo circuits. Find them new homes or let the truly bad cases go peacefully. It's something I really wanted to do."

"What's stopping you from moving to Dallas and doing it anyway?"

She gave him a startled look. "Hmm? Oh, I didn't give it up because of Devon. My friend, Nicole, who runs the ranch, will have to close it. Her funding source dried up. We tried an online fundraiser, and my dad and I donated as much as we could, but it wasn't enough. I'm trying to figure out how to help her, because she's doing good things."

Ross knew from experience exactly how horses could be abused, sometimes from ignorance, but he didn't consider that an excuse. He also knew that horses finished with their racing life were sometimes abandoned, or taken out, shot, and left for the buzzards. There were plenty of shitheads out there who had no business being anywhere near horses.

"Can she relocate?" he asked.

"I hope so. I'd like to bring her to Riverbend, or at least nearby—there's more room out here. Part of Nicole's problem is encroachment. New developments surround her, and they're trying to knock her off the property, which she doesn't own— she leases it. Pretty soon the owner is going to realize how much money he can make selling to developers, and that will be the end of that."

Callie's eyes were starry, and she balled her fists, her pie forgotten. Ross was glad to see her adamance. Too many people believed Callie was hiding in her daddy's house, moping, and Ross admitted he'd believed that too. He hadn't seen her around after he'd left her, wet and in her wedding gown, inside her front door. Not until today.

"Why don't you talk it over with my mom?" Ross asked. "Get yourself to the barbecue and corner her over the hot dogs. It's the kind of thing she'd be interested in. My family runs a nonprofit to help start-ups in Riverbend."

"Really?" The hope in Callie's eyes drove away her shyness. "Sure she wouldn't mind? That would be great."

The beautiful Callie Jones returned, her face flushed, her smile flashing, hands waving as she talked.

The untouchable debutante was now right across the table from him, pouring out her heart. The warmth in Ross grew, igniting the spark that had never died.

He let Callie talk—about the rehab ranch, about horses— as she absently ate the pie, smearing more cream on her lips. Ross listened, interested but also distracted by the need gripping his body.

Her ex had to have been crazy. What idiot would desert this woman because she'd been behind schedule? Ross would have waited days for her, sleeping under the altar in case she showed up in the night.

"I'm sorry," Callie said. Ross snapped his attention back to her as she laid her fork on her empty plate. "I've been running on. I can't believe I ate all that cream. Extra miles for me."

Ross raised his brows. "Jogging?"

"Riding. My sisters jog. I get bored after five minutes and my knees hurt. On a horse, though, I can go for hours. The ranch is huge. I can get lost out there. Be alone."

"You love it," Ross said. "Your dad's ranch."

"Of course I love it. Don't you love your family's place? I wish I was a man so I could run it with him."

Ross did have great fondness for Circle C Ranch and his memories there. He'd taken a town job for his own reasons.

"Why do you have to be a man?" he asked in true puzzlement. "My mom has run Circle C for more than twenty years, on her own at first, until my brothers and I were old enough to help out."

Callie shrugged. "My family is very traditional. Men run the business. Women join the right sorority and get married." She let out a laugh. "Not that my sisters went for that. Montana has a degree in astronomy and she's teaching courses at UT. She's not a professor yet—she's doing post-doc work. You've heard that Evelyn's singing in Austin—recording songs and trying to sell them. I'm the only one who took the traditional route. I wanted to go to vet school at A&M, but you kind of have to be brilliant, like Anna, to get in. I learned to accept a while back that I'm not brilliant. But I'm good with horses, so the rehab ranch was a godsend … And I'm talking too much *again*. Ross, you have to learn to tell me to stop."

Ross couldn't keep the satisfaction from his heart. Telling him to learn to stop her meant that she intended to be in this kind of situation again.

"I should go." Callie sounded full of regret, another good sign.

"I'll walk you out." Ross signaled for the bill, which Mrs. Ward's daughter brought, setting it squarely in front of Ross.

Callie reached for her purse.

"Don't you dare," Ross said. "Me taking out Callie Jones will make me a hero. Don't ruin it by having us go dutch." He held up a hand as she opened her mouth to argue. "You can take me out next time."

Callie stared at him, lips parted, then she gave him a nod and set the purse on her lap. "All right," she said softly.

Ross's hands shook as he rummaged in his wallet for cash, including enough for a very generous tip.

There was going to be a next time.

CALLIE TRIED NOT TO BE NERVOUS AS SHE PARKED HER Mercedes, superbly fixed by K.D., Ross's recommended mechanic, in the gravel lot roped off for the Circle C Annual Summer Barbecue.

She hadn't promised Ross she'd come, but she'd made up her mind to talk about the rehab ranch with his mother. Olivia Campbell was a well-respected and formidable woman, famous for her charitable works. Her advice about the rehab ranch would be invaluable. Callie also insisted on paying for a ticket. Mrs. Campbell didn't need to give her a free ride.

Callie didn't let herself admit the other reason she'd come. She pretended not to scan the crowd for Ross, not to look for his tall body, dark hair, and flashing smile.

When they'd left the diner, he'd politely walked her to her car, where they'd stood for almost another half hour, talking about everything and nothing.

After too many curious Riverbenders had walked past them, heads swiveling to catch every detail, Ross had opened the car door for her, made certain she'd settled in, and shut the door again, waiting to watch her drive off.

Not because he was a possessive asshole, Callie had realized as she'd glided away, returning Ross's wave. Because he cared.

Devon had never once listened to her like Ross had in Mrs. Ward's diner. Ross had fixed his complete attention on her, asking about her interests and taking in her answers. Devon's eyes had always glazed whenever Callie brought up the rehab ranch, and after a while, he hadn't even bothered with a, "That's nice, honey."

Callie gazed across the many cars to the long lines of barbecue pits, smoke wafting over the open grassland. What must be the entire population of Riverbend and surrounding towns drifted around the grills and the Campbell house, or headed into the field where tables and benches had been set up. A band tested sound equipment on a shaded stage at the far end.

Callie's heart thumped when she thought she spotted Ross, then it fell back to dull thuds when she saw that the man was not *her* Campbell. Tyler, next up in age, was plenty good-looking—all the girls had yearned after him in school—but he wasn't Ross.

Before Callie could analyze the thoughts in her head, her cell phone rang.

She dragged the phone out of her purse, and her eyes widened when she saw the name on the screen.

"Trina?" she said into it. "What the hell? I haven't heard from you in months!"

Her best friend hadn't called her since the day Callie had fled the church. The one person she'd thought she'd be able to talk to hadn't answered the phone or returned any of Callie's calls.

Callie had given up on Trina after the first couple of weeks, resigned to losing every part of the life she thought she'd built in Dallas.

"Hey, Callie." Trina sounded angry, but her voice was even, controlled. "Devon wants to talk to you."

Chapter Six

"D evon?" Callie said in bewilderment, then outrage slammed through her. "Why? I mean why *now*? He hasn't said one word to me since he ditched me. Neither have you."

"Can you blame him? Why didn't you go after him? Why didn't you call and explain? I can't believe you just let him hang like that. We were going to have so much fun, and now that's all gone."

Callie stared into the distance as Trina's words jabbed her like electric shocks.

She'd taken Ross's advice and not called Devon. Ross had been right that Callie's crime of tardiness was far less severe than Devon's act of dumping Callie, in her wedding dress, in front of her family, her friends, and the entire community.

Weeks had passed, but Devon remained silent. After a few days of crying alternating with fury, Callie's sisters and parents helplessly trying to make her feel better, then a couple weeks of out-and-out depression, Callie had decided it was over. She'd at first imagined Devon would call, and they'd fight it out, but obviously he hadn't thought it worth his time. She and her sisters and mom had sent back all the wedding gifts, then Evelyn and Montana had gone home, back to their lives, as should be.

Callie had let Devon go. Moved on. One reason she'd made herself meet Ross at the diner the other night was to take a positive step in her new life.

"He wants to talk, does he?" Callie asked, amazed at both her rage and how calm her voice remained.

"Yes. Let him, Callie," Trina said. "Let's fix this."

"It's kinda late for that, don't you think? He's had what, nearly three months to explain why the hell he had a temper tantrum and stomped off? It wasn't my fault I was late, which I would have explained, but no one gave a shit. Including you." Callie abruptly realized she hurt worse about Trina shunning her than about Devon—Trina had been her friend, her rock, through college and her years in Dallas. "You're my best friend. I thought you'd call or come see me right away, that you'd help me cope."

"You forget, my husband is *Devon's* best friend." Trina's voice held tears. "I couldn't betray them."

Callie rubbed her aching forehead. Brett and Devon were closer than brothers, and she'd looked forward to that closeness between all four of them. The Four Musketeers, Brett called them. Cliché, but it felt good to be included.

"Trina, I'm really sorry you're upset." Callie forced her voice to steady. "Of course I wouldn't want to cause trouble between you and Brett. I've had a lot of time to think it over, and I've decided Devon is out of my life. Whoever's fault it is doesn't matter anymore. We had a lot of fun, but it's done now. Doesn't mean you and I can't still be friends."

"Will you just talk to him?"

Callie let out a sigh. "I'll think about it. I'll call him in a couple days. I have a lot going on at the moment."

Trina made a startled noise. "No, I mean talk to him *right now*. He's here with us."

Callie jerked the phone from her ear, as though Devon himself had appeared next to her. *No, no, no.* Not ready. She felt sick. Not for another ten years at least.

"I'm really busy," she said quickly to Trina. "I'm at a thing. Talking to people about funding the rehab ranch."

"You and that damned ranch," Trina said. "This is your *marriage.* Priorities, Callie? I'm handing him the phone."

Before Callie could throw her cell into the grass, Devon's tones floated to her. "Callie? I need to see you."

"What for?" Callie stood rigidly, her fingers locked in place. "You had two and a half months to see me."

"I know, but I—" Devon cleared his throat. He had a deep voice, but with harsh notes she'd never noticed before. "I had to go on a business trip. That's one reason I was so mad at you for being late. I would have had to push everything around because we wouldn't have been finished in time. But that's done. We need to talk."

"Wait, you're saying you left me at the church because you needed to take a *business trip*? What about our honeymoon? Was that the same trip?"

"Killing two birds with one stone," Devon said. "You know it's my way. If I can book a private beach house on the Gulf Coast *and* get some meetings in, why not?"

He hadn't mentioned a thing about their getaway being part of a business deal.

"So you went down to Padre Island anyway?" Callie demanded.

"Why wouldn't I? I stood to bring a million-dollar investment into the firm."

"Oh, I'm so glad. You dumped me at the altar but you got a million dollars. I can see that's a fair trade."

"I *didn't* get the deal," Devon snapped. "And I didn't get married."

"Two birds with one stone, sounds like."

"Damn it." Devon drew a deep breath. "I didn't call you to fight. I want to try again."

"Marrying or getting your million-dollar deal?"

"Both."

The answer, perfectly honest, made Callie stop breathing. She couldn't even yell, *What?*

"Callie? You there, honey?"

"Yes." She managed through her clenched teeth.

"The investors had been looking forward to meeting you, heard so much about you. Your dad is well known down there. Caleb Jones, the multi-millionaire rancher, an old-fashioned, good old boy Texan, with three beautiful daughters. They wanted to see *you*, not me." Devon huffed a condescending laugh.

"Let me get this straight," Callie said, her words forced. "You want to get back with me and have us get married, and then head down to South Padre so I can sweet-talk a potential client into handing you his business?"

"What I want is you," Devon said. "But, yeah, I need you to help me land this deal. If I don't, I might lose my job. So, let's do this, Callie. You *owe* me."

For a fraction of a second, just one, Callie felt sorry for him. Devon's impatience and bad judgment had lost him a deal that his firm of stockbrokers had obviously truly wanted. And now his job might be in peril because of it.

The fraction of a second passed. "I owe *you*?" Callie shouted. "I was ready to give up my whole life for you, without much left over for myself. And you say I owe *you*?"

She jabbed her thumb to the red button to disconnect the call. The screen went black, but she needed a more satisfying ending.

Her family home had an old-fashioned dial landline telephone left over from the sixties. Her mom kept it for the nostalgia, and it still worked. Slamming that heavy plastic receiver down in anger helped a lot with closure. Cellphones just weren't the same.

Callie screamed and hurled her phone away as hard as she could.

It pinged off Ross's chest. His blue eyes widened as the phone thumped into him and dropped to the grass. "That happy to see me, are you?"

Callie stared at him for one mortifying moment before she hurled herself across the two feet separating them, flung her arms around him, and kissed him on the mouth.

Ross caught Callie as she crashed against him. He let her smooth lips part his, and then came a jolt of pure pleasure when her tongue swept into his mouth.

He tasted fire and strength, rage and need. Her hair was warm from the sunshine, falling from her ponytail to spill over his hand. Her body beneath her thin pink shirt and jeans was supple as it swayed into him.

Ross cupped Callie's chin, fully engaging with the kiss. Her breath touched his cheek and her hand went to his shoulder, fingers biting down.

She fit against him nicely, Ross holding her with one arm behind her back. Her hips moved against his thighs, and he knew she'd feel the ridge behind his jeans, the one that made him pull her closer.

Her mouth was hot, filling him with heat, her body swaying gently with the kiss.

She'd kissed him because she was pissed off at whomever had made her throw the phone — he could guess what, or who, the call was about. He'd only seen that look on her face once, and that was when she'd found out her fiancé had taken off and left her.

But so what? Whatever reason Callie had for kissing him,

Ross wasn't about to argue. The kiss didn't care. It was sweet, hot, beautiful.

Callie made a little noise in her throat. Ross answered it by deepening the kiss, tasting her mouth, pressing his hand into the small of her back. Her hips rocked into him, her knee bending to let her foot slide along his leg.

A breeze touched them, trying and failing to cool the Texas heat. It stirred Callie's hair, satin on his hand. Her chest was tight against his, her breasts soft. Ross remembered how her bridal gown had cupped her, showing him a nice amount of cleavage, tantalizing him with what was below the silk. Breasts were beautiful things.

"Whoo-eee!"

The call split the air, and Callie jerked her head up, eyes wide.

Manny, on his way to the barbecues, waved his arm, his grin huge. Ross, without embarrassment, waved back. Manny leapt and punched the air, then he landed and continued toward the smoke, his seventeen-year-old stomach focused on only one thing.

"Damn it," Callie whispered.

Ross kept his arms around her. She rested her hands on his chest as though wanting to push him away, but she remained in place.

"Don't apologize," Ross said, voice hard. "Don't tell me you didn't mean it. It was a kiss. A great one. Let's leave it at that."

Callie stared at him, her blue eyes full of anger and worry, but also desire. She drew a long breath, which pressed her breasts more firmly against him.

"All right," she said softly.

Ross eased his hold, and Callie stepped back. But she waited, not moving, as he bent to retrieve her phone and purse. She tucked away the phone, then looked nonplussed when he stuck out his arm.

"Hungry?" he asked. "Grant's really good with the grill."

Callie's mouth relaxed into a smile. "Sure." She slid her hand under his arm and let him lead her onward.

The desire he'd seen gave him hope. Ross would have to work at getting rid of her anger and worry, and fan the desire into something special.

MANNY JUDD LOOKED INTO THE KEEN BLUE EYES OF GRANT Campbell and held his plate a little higher. "I'll have mine medium well."

Grant moved his tongs to a thick piece of meat and turned it over. "Didn't you just grab a steak like five minutes ago?"

Manny contrived an innocent look. "I'm really hungry."

Grant frowned, not believing him, but he lifted another steak and slapped it onto Manny's plate. "Don't eat so fast this time."

"Thanks!" Manny zipped away, grabbed fork and knife and napkin from their bins, and forced his way onto the end of a picnic table just beyond the line of barbecue pits.

The first steak had been put into a Styrofoam to-go box Manny had procured the last time he'd been to the diner. Mrs. Ward hadn't said a word when he'd taken it from the stack behind her counter.

The steak waited for him in a cooler he'd stashed under a tree, securely sealed against bugs and critters. He'd have steak for dinner tomorrow. He'd find a way to get some big slices of pie in there too.

A shadow fell over him as he stuffed the sirloin into his mouth. The meat was meltingly tender, and he rolled it around on his tongue.

"This is really good," Manny said to the shadow — Grant — around the mouthful. "Doesn't even need steak sauce."

Manny was joking — the best way to piss off a Texas cook was to reach for the steak sauce.

"Good to know." Grant slid into the seat opposite Manny, which someone had vacated. "What are you doing here, anyway?"

Manny chewed another bite. "Don't you have meat to grill?"

Grant shrugged. "Adam took over. You know, my mom lets anyone in the county come, but only if they buy a ticket. The money goes to charity."

"So? How do you know I didn't buy a ticket?"

"Because they're two hundred dollars," Grant said patiently.

Manny stared at him, mouth open. "Two hundred bucks for a steak? Man. Rich people are crazy."

"So what are you doing here?" Grant prodded.

"Ross said I could come." Manny spoke quickly. Sounded more plausible that way.

"Yeah?" The word rang with skepticism.

"Don't you believe me?"

Grant shot him a sudden grin. "I don't have to. I'll ask him myself. Ross!"

Ross and Callie were strolling toward the table. Callie had her hand on Ross's arm. Progress. *Definite* progress, as had been that kiss in the parking lot.

Grant rose. Manny hopped up too—that was the polite thing to do when a lady was present, and Callie was seriously a lady.

"Manny." Callie sent him her warm smile. "Great to see you."

How could Ross not already be running away to Vegas with her? If the girls at school were more like Callie, instead of —*Eww, it's that Judd kid. Get him away from me*—he'd be more motivated to attend.

"Callie." Manny played it casual. "Ross."

"So, he's your guest?" Grant asked, giving Ross a cue.

Grant was cool. He didn't just come out and haul Manny away. He was giving Ross a chance be cool too.

Ross, the asshole, scowled and opened his mouth to have Manny kicked out.

Callie spoke before he could. "He's with me. I'll cover his ticket."

Ross's scowl deepened, but Grant laughed. "You're one lucky shit, Manny."

"You shouldn't do that," Ross told her.

"What, be nice to someone?" Callie released his arm. "Can't help it. Smells good. I'm ready to eat." She sauntered toward the end of the line, lifting a plate as she went.

Manny hid his glee as Ross watched her go, his gaze traveling down her body. He had it bad.

"That's not how you win a lady," Manny told him. "Let her be an angel."

"She's fine." Ross fixed his steely gaze on Manny. "What I don't want is *you* taking advantage of her. She's too nice for her own good."

Manny's quick anger rose. "I'm not taking advantage!" Was he? Manny wasn't sure. He'd have to think about it.

Grant cut in. "You and Callie?" he asked Ross. "I heard a rumor you took her out to the diner, but I didn't believe it."

"There is no me and Callie," Ross began.

"She calls, he comes running," Manny said, bouncing on the balls of his feet. "And he was kissing her in the parking lot just now."

"Yeah?" Grant looked impressed. "A Jones girl. Way to go, little brother."

"Don't call her a Jones girl," Ross growled. "Show some respect."

Grant gave Manny a conspiratorial look. "Respect. Kissing. She calls and he rushes to her. He brings her to Mom's barbecue ... I think we have some serious seriousness going on. What'd you think?"

"Yep." Manny nodded. "Serious seriousness."

"Give it a rest, Grant," Ross said wearily.

"Why? My baby brother is getting some action."

Manny didn't think Ross's face could get any darker. "There is no action," Ross said firmly. "Grow the hell up, Grant."

Grant wasn't cowed. "Well, if you took her somewhere fancier than Mrs. Ward's, maybe there'd be more action involved. A lady likes to be wined and dined."

"I keep trying to tell him," Manny said.

"Shit, the pair of you." Ross took a step closer to Manny. "I do *not* want any of this dumbass talk getting back to Callie." He glanced to her as she leaned toward Adam at the grill, charming him as easily she charmed everyone else. "Manny, you finish up your lunch and take a hike. Got it?"

Manny's disappointment hit him hard, but he'd learned long ago to hide his feelings. "I can't go yet. I haven't had any pie."

The tables were just being set up—Mrs. Ward, her daughter, and Carter's wife, Grace, started to carry out the pies.

"Fine. Have your pie, and then go."

Sweet. Manny would make sure at least one slice of each kind made it into his cooler.

Callie was heading their way, her plate loaded. "It all looked so good, I had to try a little of everything. Manny, mind if I sit with you?"

Grant sent Ross a significant look as Callie took the seat Grant had vacated, the only empty place at the long table. Callie gave Manny a big smile.

Manny knew then that Ross so needed this woman. She'd take Ross to bed and make him happy, and he'd calm down and leave Manny the hell alone.

Because if he didn't leave Manny alone, things could get dangerous—for Ross. Ross was a diligent cop, which made him the enemy of a lot of really bad people.

As much as Ross gave Manny hell, Manny kind of liked him. Ross could've had Manny locked up so tight he wouldn't get out until he was eighty, but he hadn't. He'd given Manny a break. More than one.

He was like the big brother Manny never had, and in spite of the way Ross bossed him around, a damn sight more reasonable than Manny's dad.

Ross needed to keep calm and let things go. Then the bad guys would cross Ross off their hit list and leave him alone.

Manny would fix up Ross and Callie, Ross would be safe, and everything would be all right. Manny gulped his food as worry hit him. Right?

WATCHING CALLIE WAS THE BEST PART OF THE BARBECUE, Ross decided. In past years, he'd come for the food and to hang out with his brothers, mom, and friends, but today, it was all about Callie.

He knew she felt awkward about facing the whole town after her ignominious wedding. She had nothing to be ashamed of, but he understood. Having everyone she'd ever known watch her be humiliated, and then either pity her or spitefully say she got what she deserved, couldn't be fun.

Ross had gone through something similar when he'd announced he wouldn't be joining his brothers in their stunt-riding shows. While trick riding had been fun as a kid, the thought of galloping around showing off, when he wasn't recovering from broken bones, wasn't his idea of a productive life.

Being sheriff's deputy in a small town would never be exactly safe—small towns and surrounding countryside attracted their share of criminals—but he preferred driving his SUV along beautiful back roads to trying to coax Buster the shithead wonder horse to do his tricks. He wanted to help people and keep them safe, not ride around arenas while spectators held their breaths, half-hoping he'd fall on his ass.

However, stunt riding had become an established Campbell tradition by the time Ross had been old enough to join his brothers in their shows. The fact that Ross had taken a low-paying, relatively thankless job handing out traffic tickets instead of basking in fame like the rest of his brothers had made the town talk. Rumors were that Ross and his brothers had had a big fight. Total bullshit circulated that he'd been caught with a brother's girlfriend, though rumor couldn't decide if the girlfriend had been Grant's, Tyler's, or Carter's.

The crap he'd gotten from the town had stung. Ross had dealt with their disapprobation by ignoring everyone the best he could until they got used to him in his uniform. Carter had taken Ross's side as well, and few people wanted to argue with Carter.

Callie was handling her reemergence with aplomb. She turned to greet people with a ready smile, a gentle handshake, hugs for women she knew. She spoke animatedly but wasn't over-eager, didn't push herself on anyone.

When Ross introduced her to his mother—they already knew each other, of course, but it was polite— *Mom, you remember Callie*—Olivia had immediately folded Callie into her arms. "Honey, I'm so sorry what happened to you. No one blames you, dear."

That was the closest Ross had seen Callie come to breaking down. She blinked away tears and then started talking about her friend's horse rehab ranch. Olivia's face lit with interest, and Ross had left them to it.

As the barbecue began to wind down, Ross met Callie on the porch of the ranch house. The day had turned unmercifully hot, and remaining guests sought shade and cool drinks under open-air tents. The band had finished and now lounged offstage, drinking beer.

"You look happy," Ross observed as Callie smiled up at him from the porch swing, glass of iced tea in hand.

"Your mom gave me some great ideas," Callie said. "I'm all set to talk to Karen Marvin, who runs your family's nonprofit. I don't know her well—what's she like?"

"She was at your wedding," Ross pointed out.

"Because my mother invited the entire town. I met her briefly, once, but I don't *know* her."

Ross thought about Karen, the hard-as-nails business-woman who had a surprising soft side, but also a yen for cowboys. She'd had a new one on her arm today, a brash young man from the rodeo circuit. "She's good at what she does. Don't expect warm, but she is efficient."

"Fine with me. My friend Nicole needs solutions, not hand-holding. I'm getting excited about it again. That feels nice, you know? After a couple months of sitting around feeling sorry for myself, I'm glad to have something to do."

It looked good on her too. Callie's face was flushed, her eyes shining.

"Taking your life into your own hands. Yep, I know all about that."

"Well." Callie abandoned her iced tea and rose, lifting her purse and hugging it to her chest. "I guess I should go."

Ross liked that she sounded reluctant. Could be that she'd had a great time today and didn't want it to end, but he hoped she felt unwillingness to leave Circle C, the Campbell family, Ross.

"Guess you should." Ross glanced down the porch. A clump of guests congregated on the far end, laughing and talking, leaving Ross and Callie relatively alone. "Except ..."

"Except?" Callie moved half an inch toward him. "Except what?"

This was embarrassing. Ross leaned closer and made himself ask. "Would you give me a ride home? I'm kind of stranded."

Chapter Seven

Of all the things Callie expected Ross to say—of all the things she *wanted* him to say—asking for a ride home wasn't it.

But he only gave her the hopeful look of a person who knew she'd be driving his way.

"Don't you have a car?" was her inane response. *Smooth, Callie.*

Ross shrugged. "I came with Grant, but he and Christina are going to spend the night. I keep my sheriff's vehicle at the station. Don't usually need a car other than that."

Callie gave him a stiff smile. "Sure."

She should add that with all he'd done for her, it would be a pleasure, but her mouth wouldn't move.

All she could do was march off the porch and make for the now mostly empty lot in the dusty field where she'd left her car.

Ross walked beside her, not hurrying. He glanced around, peering at shadows, craning his head to look toward the stables and riding rings. Callie thought she knew what he searched for —or rather, *who*.

"I saw Manny leave," Callie told him. "He hitched a ride in the back of a pickup."

"Good. I hope he went home and stayed there."

Callie had watched the youth fetch a cooler from under a clump of trees, stash something inside, and then rush out and leap into the bed of Ray Malory's pickup. She didn't like to say anything about the cooler—Manny had obviously been taking extra food home so he'd have something to eat for the next day or so.

"He's a nice kid," Callie said.

Ross shot her a look. "Deep down, he is. He grew up too much on his own. No one to guide him."

"You could always adopt him," Callie said with a smile.

Ross blinked. "He's seventeen and eleven months."

"You could be his adoptive uncle. Or big brother."

"And let him live with me? You think that because you haven't seen my apartment. It's a postage stamp."

"A postage stamp. Do people still say that?"

"*I* do." They reached her car. Callie clicked her key fob to unlock it, and the next instant, Ross opened the door for her, like the gentleman he was. He shut the door after she seated herself and moved to the passenger side to slide in.

"Drive fast," he said, scanning the horizon. "I don't like the look of those clouds."

"The sheriff's deputy is telling me to speed?" Callie pulled out of the lot and drove sedately down the winding lane that led to the highway. Thick dark clouds had gathered in the north, bearing down on the rolling grasslands. "Anyway, clouds always look like that in Texas."

"Like any minute we could have a hailstorm?" Ross said. "Or a light sprinkling? Or a tornado? Whatever nature decides."

"You worry a lot, you know that?" Callie spoke lightly, but she also eyed the thunderheads in trepidation. Storms blew up fast, and while the Hill Country didn't always receive the crazy weather West Texas or North Texas could, it might be bad enough.

She turned onto the highway that led into Riverbend. Most of the other guests had gone, and the road was empty.

"Nice car," Ross said, leaning back in the seat. "K.D. did a good job."

"He did." Callie stroked the blue-gray steering wheel. "This is my first car, did you know? I bought it with the first money I ever made. It's a good car, so I keep it up."

"An S-class. Good choice." He chuckled. "Good salary."

"I was working for a stockbrokers' in Dallas." *Where I met Devon.* Callie had no inclination to speak his name, so she left him out of it. "Not the job I envisioned for the rest of my life, but the money was decent."

Devon hadn't wanted her to continue working after they got engaged. Bad idea for two people in love to work in the same office, he'd claimed. But now she understood he'd wanted her to become the trophy wife, waiting at home, ready to impress his clients.

"What does a stockbroker do, exactly?" Ross asked as the first fat drops of rain fell. "I know about the scammy ones, the boiler rooms."

"Legit stockbrokers do a lot of market research," Callie said, babbling to keep her mind off Devon. "They figure out what's hot and what's dying off, what's a fairly safe bet versus something that will flare up and tank. A good broker can really help people. Money is a responsibility—you have to take care of it, or it will vanish. I don't mean because you blow it too fast, but if you have it in the wrong kind of account, say, fees will eat it up, or it can get taxed to nothing."

"What's wrong with buying land?" Ross gazed at the hills around them, green with summer. "Safest investment, right?"

"Not necessarily. If you buy the wrong property at the wrong time, and the market crashes, you're paying tons of money for land that's worth little. It can ruin you."

The rain came down harder, and Callie slowed and turned on her wipers to the highest setting. She shivered as she remembered the storm on her wedding day, and how Ross's SUV had cut through it, coming to her rescue.

"Sounds like you gave out good advice," Ross said.

"The job can be soul-sucking, though," Callie said. "Clients trust you with everything they have. You have to explain the realistic returns, which are not the huge amounts boiler room scammers promise. And when the market changes unexpectedly, or people don't take your advice to pull out in time, they can lose everything. It's not so bad with the billionaires who are playing with a hundred thousand here, a hundred thousand there, but some people are trying to build college funds or buy a house for the family. It can break your heart."

"Which is why you want to switch to ranching. Because, you know, no one ever broke their heart over that."

"Oh, I realize it's risky. But it seems more—I don't know—personal. Maybe because I grew up around ranches and horses. It's natural to me."

Ross grinned. "Yeah, the pretty cotillion dress and calling cards were so natural."

"Are you making fun of me?" Callie lowered her brows, but in reality she liked his teasing. Devon never teased. Never joked, except when he disparaged others in a slow drawl. To think, Callie used to believe Devon witty, when it turned out he was just mean. "It taught me how to be polite. Is that so bad? Maybe you should take lessons."

"Learn to drink tea and quirk my pinky?" Ross demonstrated. "If I do that in Sam's bar, I'll get pulverized."

Callie laughed. It felt good to laugh at nothing. She hadn't done that in far too long.

The rain was streaming down by the time Callie, following Ross's directions, drove to the narrow alley behind buildings around the town square. The tiny artery between the busi-

nesses on the square and the next street contained small
garages with just enough space to pull into and out of them.

Callie stopped in front of one of the garages, and Ross
opened his door. "Come upstairs."

She wanted to—she felt the pull to dash inside with him
out of the rain. She also knew it was too soon, too fast. Her
heart sped as she drew a breath.

Ross slid out to yank the garage door up and then ducked
back inside the car. "It's coming down too hard for you to drive
safely. I do not want to get a call that you've gone off the road
again, or hear that some other driver has hit you and you're in
an ambulance."

His expression was grim. This was Ross the deputy talking,
the one who'd helped pull the injured, the dying, out of cars on
Texas's dangerous highways.

It was true that the drivers of River County, used to mostly
fair weather, went a little loopy as soon as the rain pelted
down. Heaven help them the rare year they had a dusting
of snow.

Caution, coupled with Callie's desire to see where Ross
lived, clinched it. She pulled slowly forward into the empty
garage.

A large chunk of the garage was taken up by a tool bench
with various metal parts lying on it, plus a grinder and a drill
press. Callie's car barely fit, but there was enough room for
each of them to open a door and slide out.

She locked her car out of habit with the key fob, though
Ross pulled the garage door closed and secured it before he led
her to a plain door that opened to a cement-floored hall. A door
at the far end presumably led to the offices in front of the
building, and a staircase with a wrought iron railing rose
straight upward.

Callie knew from many years driving around the square
that the office in front belonged to the lawyers Long and
Emmons, who had been drawing up wills, doing land and

tenant agreements, representing lawsuits, and processing divorces in Riverbend for generations.

As this was Saturday, they'd shut for the weekend. The businesses to either side of it, one a bicycle shop, the other an artist supply store begun by a recent arrival to Riverbend, were also closed for the day.

The staircase led to a landing that held another door, which Ross opened with a key.

"I rent the upper two floors," he said as he led her into a small space with large windows that faced the square. "Living area here, bedroom upstairs."

This row of buildings was at least a hundred and so years old, erected when the square had been first established around the courthouse. The shops had been renovated and remodeled several times, the upper floors turned into offices or apartments.

The space Callie found herself in was small, as Ross had said, but airy, with a kitchen tucked against the back wall and partitioned from the living room by a small breakfast bar. Mismatched furniture clustered around a television, and the area under the front windows contained a single bench with a spindled back, an antique by the look of it.

Near the kitchen, on the wall shared with the next apartment over, an open staircase rose to the upper level.

"Bathroom's up there if you need it," Ross said, heading for the kitchen.

Rain beat on the windows, hard enough that Callie could hear it on the roof upstairs. In the kitchen Ross ran water, and then came the gurgle of a coffeemaker and the first aroma of hot liquid on ground beans.

The rain had turned the air cool—cool for a Hill Country July, anyway—and coffee would be refreshing.

"Nice place," Callie said. "Cozy."

"Could use some fixing up." Ross leaned on the breakfast bar from the kitchen side, his rolled-up sleeves revealing brown arms tight with muscle. "But I'm not here much. I work a lot."

"You sure do. I see you driving around, on the lookout for bad guys."

Callie moved to the windows, making certain she stayed far enough back so a passing motorist wouldn't notice her, though with the rain, probably no one could see up here anyway. Still, gossip that she'd been in Ross's apartment would rocket around town in minutes.

When Ross didn't answer, Callie turned back. "Sorry, did I say something wrong? I was joking."

"There are more bad guys than you'd think." Ross's tone was serious. "They come to places like Riverbend because they believe they can hide. Some guys I'm after right now are in White Fork, living in a middle-class residential area. Lying low. We're pretty sure who they are, but they're too canny to do anything overt—they're not cooking meth in the back shed—but they are dealers, and they are dangerous. Getting to them isn't easy."

"Oh." Callie blinked. "I didn't know that."

"Not many do. It's another reason I don't want you driving around on empty roads. These guys—and women—are dick-heads, and they don't like me. They expect me to look the other way while they carry on." Ross snapped his mouth shut, as though stopping himself from saying more.

Callie had the sudden desire to make him feel better. She moved to the kitchen island, keeping it between them, and laid her hand on his fist. "Guess they're not used to honest cops."

"No." The one word was short, but Ross didn't look at her. His gaze was on their hands, her slim fingers resting on his blunt ones.

"Well, *I* like honest cops," she said softly. "Especially ones who stop and help a woman in the rain."

When Ross finally looked at her, the heat in his eyes made her breath catch. "Just doing my job, ma'am."

Without lifting her hand, Callie slid around the counter to him. At the same time, he started out from behind. They met in the middle, the counter's edge pressing into Callie's hip.

"Here I thought you were being nice," she said to fill the silence. Even the rain had quieted, but Callie didn't want to point that out.

"Couldn't bypass a damsel in distress," Ross said softly. "I'd never forgive myself."

"Then you ran away with the bride."

"Not far. But I couldn't resist." Ross touched her cheek, his strong finger surprisingly gentle.

"Should have. The whole town's talking about us."

His fingertip moved across her cheekbone and down the side of her nose to her lips. "Does that bother you?"

"Right now? Not at all."

"Good."

Ross drew her forward with his fingers under her chin and kissed her firmly on the lips.

Chapter Eight

C allie stilled as Ross's kiss wrapped around her.
When she'd kissed him in the parking lot, she'd leapt at him in desperation, her anger spurring her on. He hadn't been repulsed — he'd held her until she'd calmed down.

This kiss was seeking, learning, coaxing. Ross's mouth was strong but his touch was light, as though he feared pushing her too hard too fast. His lips were smooth, like the softest bed sheets, and tasted of salt, spice, *him*.

Callie stepped closer in his embrace, his belt buckle pressing into her abdomen. All the Campbells wore a huge buckle with *Circle C* on it, a badge that had earned them both envy and derision back in school. Girls would debate on which Campbell brother had the largest and the hardest, and dared each other to find out.

Callie had to say she thought Ross would win.

He turned them so Callie's back was to the counter, and then her feet left the floor. Ross lifted her to sit on the granite top, and a moment later they were at eye level, her legs loosely around his.

Ross eased back from the kiss, though it hadn't gone beyond the brushing of lips. He said nothing and didn't move, which allowed her time to study him.

A scar pulled the edge of his left eyebrow, white in the deep tan of his face, which came from a lifetime under Texas sunshine. His straight nose and square chin made his features regular and handsome, and he wore his dark hair cut into a tight buzz so it wouldn't be in his way. Most of all, his Campbell blue eyes, like twilit skies, gazed straight at her.

Callie read the desire in him, which pulsed heat through her body. Her own rising desire met and matched it.

She'd touched no one since Devon—and not even Devon for a while, because they'd gone their separate ways during the crazy wedding preparations. But it wasn't only physical need that made Callie lean into Ross and seek his kiss again.

She'd been bitterly lonely, nursing anger, hurt, betrayal, mortification. She'd made a bad choice, and she'd hidden out in embarrassment, licking her wounds, avoiding people. Callie regretted the years she'd wasted trying to be the perfect couple with Devon, realizing now that any time she'd stepped out of line, he'd been there to admonish her, tell her she was in the wrong, warn her to do better.

Abusive husbands did that, she knew, but at the time, she hadn't seen the signs. She'd thought it her fault when shit happened, that he'd awakened her to her shortcomings. She'd figured no one had pointed them out before because none had been brave enough to tell Callie and her sisters that they weren't exemplary.

Ross didn't give a shit whether or not she was perfect. What she saw in his eyes was naked need, for *her*. Not to see whether she was the ideal woman, but because he was interested in *Callie*.

She'd seen the same flash in his eyes that long-ago day when he'd walked up to her, hands sliding into his pockets while he asked her casually for her Spanish homework.

She'd seen, and hadn't believed. So many years had passed —if they'd understood what they were feeling back then, had known what to do with it, her life might have been very different.

"Ross," she whispered.

"Shh." He touched his forehead to hers. "Don't say anything. Let's enjoy this moment."

He thought she wanted to stop him, to tell him this was a mistake. The truth was, she'd said his name to hear the sound of it, and to let him know she was just as hungry.

She rested one hand on his chest, pushing at him until he lifted his head. She caught his mouth in a kiss, her eyes open to share her heart.

Ross jumped, and everything changed.

Something electric shot between them as Ross closed hard hands around her arms. Callie swore sparks leapt from his body to hers, arcs joining them in crackling need.

Thunder boomed outside and kept on rolling. Maybe they'd just been struck by lightning.

Not likely, and Callie didn't care. She moved her hand to his shirt buttons and started to pop them open.

Ross deepened the kiss. His lips parted hers, his tongue sweeping inside her mouth, stirring more sparks.

The counter dug into her hips. Callie pulled Ross closer with her legs, unable to stop her noise of satisfaction when he stepped rigidly against her.

Heat pounded through her. The rising scent of brewing coffee seeped around them, making her imagine mornings waking to breakfast and Ross. He'd look good wrapped in nothing but early sunshine.

One of Ross's buttons slid from a hole, then another, and another. Callie spread the shirt, to find a body-hugging T-shirt beneath and that his heart was pounding as much as hers.

Callie bunched her fingers in the T-shirt, wishing it gone so she could touch his skin. Ross ran his hands down her back, scooping her closer, cupping her backside.

The coffeemaker beeped, its gurgle ceasing in a sigh of steam. Ross broke from Callie long enough to slam his hand to its *off* button and return to her.

His eyes were dark, his chest rising with each harsh breath. He shrugged out of the unbuttoned shirt and enclosed her in his arms again, only the soft tee between them now.

Callie wrapped herself around him, abandoning all for his kiss, letting worry and anger drift away. All that mattered was Ross, his warmth, his strong arms, his kiss easing everything bad in the world.

When Ross lifted his head and looked at her, his eyes were filled with wanting, and hope. Callie gazed back at him, trying to convey the same hope. His bedroom was up a flight of stairs, and no one in the world knew where they were.

Ross kissed her again. This time, their mouths met in slow deliberation, warm with passion. As another rumble of thunder rolled over the land, Ross slid his hand over Callie's waist and cupped her breast.

She was burning. He stroked with his palm, Callie's nipple rising and tightening to his caress. She wore a satin bra under her thin shirt, and its fabric wasn't nearly thick enough to keep Ross out. She felt every stroke of his fingers, the heat of his touch, the press of the heel of his hand as he continued to kiss her.

Lightning flashed outside the windows, but it was nothing to the fire *inside*.

Ross undid the three buttons at the top of Callie's shirt. The buttons were mostly decorative but did part her collar enough so Ross could draw the shirt halfway down her arms.

Callie laughed. "Let me," she said, then before she could stop herself, she pulled the shirt up and off.

Now she was sitting on the counter in Ross Campbell's

apartment in nothing but her jeans and a hot pink bra. Ross's smile of appreciation warmed her all over.

"You're beautiful, Callie. You always have been."

Callie tried to shrug, to make a joke of it. Anything to keep him from seeing how much she wanted to shiver, or melt into a puddle, or launch herself at him again. "Nah. Evelyn is the beautiful one."

"Not where I'm standing." Ross's deep drawl was a caress.

He cupped her cheek, thumb hot on her cheekbone. A moment later, he took a step back and skimmed off his own shirt.

Callie allowed herself a slow, appreciative scan of his body. Ross obviously worked out—all the deputies went to the gym around the corner. His arms were darkly tanned from driving under bright skies all day, but the rest of him was a touch lighter, which would be comical if he weren't so beautiful.

Ross had never had the giant physique of the football players who'd wanted to date the Jones sisters and be homecoming king to their queen, but he had lean, compact tightness. His sculpted chest was dusted with black hair, his shoulders capped with muscle.

He also wasn't as tall as his four older brothers, but Callie did not find this a detraction. An asset, she thought, as she did not have to crane her neck to the breaking point to kiss him.

Ross leaned his fists on either side of her. "I want to take you upstairs," he said. "You all right with that?"

Callie tried to answer, but her tongue wouldn't work. She settled for a nod.

Ross's smile renewed her fires. Lightning flashed outside, followed immediately by a *boom*.

"Close," Ross said. He glanced at the police scanner and radio plugged in next to the coffee maker. If that lightning bolt had struck a house or car, he'd be called.

The radio remained silent, a very low hiss the only clue it was on.

Ross scooped Callie from the counter and against him. His next kiss stole her breath, and then Ross released her, snatched up their shirts in one hand, and led Callie to the stairs.

CALLIE WAS LETTING HIM TAKE HER UP TO HIS BEDROOM. Ross decided not to think too hard about that, because he'd do something stupid like shout in joy, do a fist pump, and probably fall down the stairs.

She smiled at him, beautiful in the pink satin that held her ample breasts, her brown and gold hair coming loose from its ponytail. He remembered catching her in the rain, when her body had been embraced by the white satin bodice. He'd appreciated the rise of her curves then, and he couldn't help sliding his hand over them now.

The staircase, polished wood with wrought iron railings that he and Tyler had built together, had never seemed so long.

The second floor loft consisted of his bedroom, with a bathroom behind a partition wall. Windows to the rear gave a view over the shorter buildings on the next street and out into the wide grasslands.

As soon as they made it to the bedroom, Ross moved from Callie, dropped their clothes onto a chair, and pulled down all the blinds.

She watched him with a look of amusement. But storm or no, Ross wasn't having the whole town look up here and see Callie in her bra.

He was glad he'd at least straightened the sheets and blankets on his bed, even if he didn't have it neatly made and decorated with the throw pillows Grace had given him. Ross had a cleaner come in once a week, because he was never home, so at least everything was dusted and the floor vacuumed.

Ross came back to Callie. Her smile vanished as he slid his arms around her and pulled her close.

The crush of her breasts against him made his breath hitch. She was softness and curves, while he was angles and lines.

He sought that softness, hands smoothing her waist down to her jeans then up to the strap of her bra. Callie touched him in return, exploring his chest, his shoulders, moving back to his flat nipples.

They tightened as much as hers did, the tingle making Ross slightly crazy. The nerve endings reached his cock, which was hard and feeling confined.

Her bra strap gave, the satin loosened, and Callie helped him slide it from her. She tossed it away with a little flourish that made him even harder.

Ross drew her to him and twirled her in a tight circle, as though they danced to a band at the bar. Callie laced her arms around his neck.

"You're seducing me, Ross Campbell." Her breath was hot on his cheek.

"I think it's the other way around." Ross nuzzled her neck, inhaling the clean scent of her.

"Really?"

Her overjoyed tone made Ross raise his head. Callie's blue eyes sparkled. "I've never seduced anyone before," she said. "It's kind of fun."

"You have me hooked." Ross kissed where he'd nuzzled and gave her a nip. Her taste shot his need high. "Up in my bedroom and everything."

"It's lovely. Nice view." She waved at the closed blinds.

"Yeah, I think so." Ross stared blatantly at her breasts, bare now, nipples dark pink, darkening even more under his scrutiny.

Callie laughed. "You're a shit."

"That's what they call me. *Ross, you little shit.*"

"You aren't so little."

"Not anymore." Ross kissed her lips, leaning into her to cup her breasts.

Satin softness met his touch. Ross wasn't sure what either of them intended, if what they'd started would go all the way, and he didn't care.

He'd learned, since he'd become a deputy, to live in the moment. Every bit of concentration went into what happened *now*. Focus could be the difference between life and death.

Ross turned that focus on Callie, kissing her as he opened the button of her jeans.

Callie brushed his hand on the way to popping his belt buckle loose. "It really is big," she murmured.

Ross started. "What?"

Callie let out a laugh. "Didn't you know all the girls in school wanted to measure your buckle?"

Ross's face heated, and his mouth went dry. "No."

Callie laughed harder, which moved her body in an enticing way. "Aw, you look so shy."

Shy? True, people said that about Ross because he was quiet—at least compared to his four loud, full-of-themselves brothers. But *quiet* was different from *shy*. Ross didn't see the need to fill up space with his own words.

"Think so?" he asked, his voice calm.

Callie nodded, her smile wide. Ross ran fingers through her hair, pulling out the band that held her ponytail in place. He wound the satin of her hair around his hand and tugged her closer for another deep kiss.

Callie's teasing evaporated as she answered his kiss with a hard one of her own.

The *Will we?* changed to *We will*.

Ross released her with reluctance but only to jerk off his boots and unzip his pants. He mashed the jeans down his legs, stepping out of them, not worrying that he probably looked like an idiot in only his socks and tight boxer briefs. He was glad they'd left her purse downstairs, so she couldn't whip out her phone and snap his picture. One share later, and he'd be a global fool.

Callie gave him a once over, the interested look in her eyes telling him she didn't think he looked like an idiot.

She was an eyeful with one arm folded across her bare stomach, a posture that lifted her full beasts. Sending him a coy look, she cocked one hip and slid down the zipper of her jeans.

Ross was against her in an instant, helping her push down the pants, his hands going into her underwear to seek her bare backside. The power of the moment wrapped around them, and all joking ceased.

A burst of lightning blared through cracks in the blinds, followed by a long, never-ending rumble. The lightning had been so bright that its absence made his bedroom all the darker.

In that instant, Callie slid off her shoes and kicked out of her jeans and her panties, which were pink to match her bra, everything falling into a pool of fabric.

Ross gathered her in his arms, turning her in their dance toward the bed, lowering her onto it. Callie leaned back on her elbows on the mattress, the most glorious sight his bedroom had ever known. Beautiful Callie, naked on his covers, her hair mussed, her blue eyes watching.

Some humor in the situation returned as Ross made a mad dash for the bathroom and scrabbled in the drawer for the box of condoms that should be there. He found one, did a quick check of the expiration date, and raced back out.

Callie was trying not to laugh at him. She'd raised one foot to brace it on the bed, unconsciously giving him a view of the glory to come.

How Ross got out of his underwear, he didn't know, but it was flying to the floor the moment before he put one knee on the bed and came over Callie. He eased her down into the mattress and dropped the foil-wrapped condom beside her.

"Aren't you going to put that on?" she asked in puzzlement.

"Not yet."

Ross didn't want this encounter to be *wham, bam, thank you, ma'am*. He wanted to savor her, draw it out, create memories of her for after she was gone.

He kissed her as he came down on her, his very hard cock resting between her thighs. She ran her hands through his hair, giving him her lovely Callie smile.

"Wow," she said softly. "I'm really here with Ross Campbell. How did I get so lucky?"

Chapter Nine

How did I get so lucky? Callie's face heated at the stupid line, but Ross's eyes warmed.

"I was thinking the same about you," he said.

Callie touched his face. Ross turned his head and kissed her palm, fanning the fires already scorching her.

When she'd been growing up Ross had been a sexy Campbell, forbidden fruit, who worked in the dust and fell off horses with his brothers for fun. *The wild Campbell boys,* every girls' parents warned. *Stay away from them. You never know what they'll do.*

One of them had enticed her into his loft... only ten miles from her home, though it might as well be a world away.

They gazed at each other for a long moment, and then past and future didn't matter. The present was all-encompassing.

Ross kissed her slowly. He drew his hand between her breasts, ran a finger around her navel, and slid his touch between her thighs.

Callie ignited. Liquid heat flowed from her, drawn by his hand. She moved on the bed, her thoughts scattered, replaced by sensation alone.

She rose to him, needing him. A groan escaped her—she'd never made a noise like *that* before. She thought she'd experienced orgasms in her life but soon realized that she'd only ever touched the tip of the iceberg.

Ross's fingers found the places that opened her, seared her. Her head went back, and she cried out as white heat blotted all other feeling. She knew nothing but wildness and Ross, as lightning flashed and thunder boomed.

Dimly she heard the rustle of foil, felt the absence of his hand. She wanted his touch back, heard herself beg for it.

The condom brushed her, but its coolness gave way as Ross filled her.

He stilled as he slid inside, opening her wider than she'd ever been in her life. He gazed down at her with eyes that held the same desire that seized her.

"Ross." Her voice was dry.

"Callie," came his whisper in return. "What you do to me …"

He thrust. Callie arched to take it, and another wave of fire flooded her. Her cries echoed through the loft and spilled down the stairwell to the space below.

Ross let out a groan that matched hers in volume. He thrust again, then rhythm took over, and they moved with it, Callie drowning in pleasure.

Thunder drowned out their cries, and hailstones hit the roof and the windows, beating hard, trying to get in. Lightning lit the room, showing her Ross in stark brightness, the reflection of him in the long mirror next to the stairs. She saw his tight body, the rise and fall of his hips, his arms bunched as he took his weight.

In the next instant, the room went dark. Callie knew nothing but Ross inside her, the warmth of his body on hers, his kisses on her face.

Nothing but Ross. She wrapped herself around him as he

continued to thrust, let feeling engulf her, and needed nothing else.

A LONG TIME LATER, ROSS WOKE. HE FELT HEAVY, EVERY molecule relaxed, his body sinking deep into the mattress.

He remembered the white hot sensation of coming inside Callie, the sound of her cries filled with joy, her fingers hard on his back. They'd rocked together for long while before Callie had collapsed, limp, her eyes heavy, her smile languid.

Ross had managed to get rid of the condom, then they'd drowsed together, touching and kissing. He'd tried to stay awake and enjoy every second, but sleep had smacked him and taken him down.

He stretched out his arm ... and found only a warm indentation where Callie had been.

Alarmed, he rose on his elbows and scanned the room.

Callie turned to him from the foot of the bed, in the act of doing up the tiny buttons on her shirt. Outside, it was quiet, the storm having moved on. Sunlight poked through the blinds, its slant indicating the long summer day drawing to a close.

"Hey," Ross said.

Callie finished buttoning. "Hey."

"It's still early," he said. "I think. How about we grab some dinner?"

"Ross."

God help him, she was going to break up with him. Let him down easy. Walk away, out of his life.

No! Something inside him shouted. *Don't let her!*

"Ross, what?" he growled.

Callie let out a breath, sorrow in her eyes. "I shouldn't have done that. I don't want this to be ..." Another breath. "You know, rebound sex."

Ross made a nonchalant gesture, though his heart was pounding like crazy. "Why does it have to be anything?"

Callie hesitated. "Because it was great, for one thing. Seriously ... great." She flushed, and Ross's heart warmed. He didn't want it to be *wham, bam, thank you, sir,* for her either. "But I don't want to hurt you," she went on in a rush. "What happened to me wasn't your fault. I don't want to use you to get over it."

Pain bit him, and Ross gave another flick of his hand to cover the sting. "Use me. I don't mind." At her startled look, he forced a smile. "Callie, we don't have to make this anything. If you're trying to feel better—well, then, I hope I made you feel better. If we're just having fun, then we're having fun. It doesn't have to mean the world changes."

She blinked. "You mean kind of like friends with benefits?"

"Naw. That's bullshit. You're different with someone you've slept with, as hard as you try to deny that. I'm hoping this means we're more than friends. Really *close* friends. But it doesn't have to be a stifling thing. You don't need that right now."

Callie swallowed, her nod quick. "You don't need that either."

"I don't know what I need," Ross said calmly, though his breathing was way too fast for the conversation. "And I don't know what *this* is. But I'm willing to hang around and find out."

"Are you?" She sounded surprised.

"Sure. But I don't want to do it by myself." Ross moved to sit on the edge of the bed, feet on the floor. He was stark naked while Callie was clothed, and that was fine with him. He could wrap himself around her and maybe make her come while she was fully dressed.

His cock jumped at the thought, and Ross rapidly thought about cold showers, snowballs, jumping into the ice tray in his freezer downstairs ...

He made himself shrug. "If this turns out to be nothing, then hey, we had a good time figuring it out. If it turns into something, then I want to be with you when we discover that."

Callie's lips parted as he fed her these ideas. Ross knew he was leaving himself wide open for her to say she wasn't interested, to thank him for the couple hours of fun and return to her world of riches and politeness, but he had to take a chance.

Her throat moved, and he was sure her next word would be *no*, and that she should go.

"All right," she stunned him by saying. "What do we do?"

Ross stood up so fast his head spun. "You let me take a shower, then we go get something to eat."

She continued to stare, and he liked that her gaze flicked down his body, giving his cock an interested glance. "Not hiding anything, you mean."

He grinned. "We're adults, we're single, we're consenting. It's our business." He gestured to the window. "Show them no one messes with a Jones."

Callie's lips twitched. "Or a Campbell?"

"Damn straight. Now, don't go anywhere. I'll be right out."

CALLIE DESCENDED TO THE LIVING ROOM WHILE THE shower pattered behind the bathroom door. The impulse to charge inside, pull back the curtain, and dive in with Ross was intense, so Callie deliberately walked down the polished staircase, out of temptation's reach.

But not far enough. Her legs were wobbly, her eyes sandy, and she needed to process what had just happened. She'd been about to sneak out, go home, and hide, when Ross had opened his eyes.

He'd regarded her, unworried, from his bed, full-length and naked, blue eyes warm with afterglow.

Don't worry about it, he'd basically said. *Let's see what happens.*

Callie had never been in a casual relationship in her life. She'd either been left alone, guys too intimidated by her family to ask her out, or in a high-pressure situation to be the perfect girlfriend. That's what she'd been raised to be, right?

Ross wasn't asking anything of her. Just dinner out, probably at the diner, then maybe back here for some more great sex.

A tightness inside her eased. She could laugh with Ross, talk about stupid things. She could be Callie, the nerdy woman who liked horses and reading, her real self. He didn't seem to mind.

She poured herself a cup of the waiting coffee, the machine having kept it warm. The bitter jolt on her tongue as she sipped woke her.

The radio crackled. "Ross?" a woman's voice called. "You there?"

Callie froze in the act of taking another sip, eyes on the police radio. Should she pick it up? She was familiar with radios because her dad used them to communicate with his hands on the far reaches of the ranch. More reliable than cell phones, usually. But this was a police frequency, which meant she had no business being on it.

"Ross? We're trying to track you down."

Callie compromised. She grabbed the radio from its charging cradle and raced upstairs with it. Ross was just snapping off the water as she ran inside the bathroom.

"Someone's looking for you."

Turned out the shower didn't have a curtain but a wall of glass blocks that separated it from the rest of the room. If she'd talked herself into coming in before, she'd have had a nice show.

Ross came around the blocks, dripping, naked, and delectable, and regarded the radio Callie thrust at him in dismay. "Damn it." He grabbed a towel and dried off his hands then tucked the towel around his middle and reached for the radio.

"Mildred? What's up?"

"Hennessy is looking for you. Hate to bug you on your day off, but there's a meeting—you're the last."

"Shit." Annoyance flushed Ross's face. "I'll be there. Give me ten. I'm just getting out of the shower."

"Gotcha," Mildred said, and the radio clicked off.

Ross set it on the counter, snatched up a second towel and rubbed it over his hair. "Sorry, Callie."

"I understand," she said, trying to stifle her disappointment. "It's work."

Ross rumbled. "It's Hennessy. He'll call these meetings spontaneously—late—just to dick with us. Sometimes it's serious police business. Sometimes it's about someone parking on the line between his space and theirs. Either way, I have to go." He discarded the second towel, his dark hair every which way, and came to her. "I can't tell you how sorry I am."

Damp hands closed around her as Ross pulled her up to him to kiss her.

He'd tasted good during sex, and afterward was definitely not bad. His lips were wet and warm from his shower, his skin smelling of soap and shaving cream.

Ross eased the kiss to its close, his gaze on her mouth. "Damn the man."

"Not your fault," Callie said softly. "No need to apologize."

"I don't mean I'm sorry because I'm taking the blame. I mean I'm damn sorry I can't spend more time with you. Take you to dinner, bring you back home, have *you* take a shower …"

"Yeah, I'm kinda sorry about all that too."

"I'm not kicking you out," Ross said. "You're welcome to stay as long as you want, drink the coffee, take a bath, fix yourself something to eat—I know how to cook, so I have actual food in my fridge. Or you can head home. Your choice."

Stay here in this cozy apartment with Ross's things around her? Or go home to the big empty house and painful memories? Hmm, tough choice. "How long you think you'll be?" Callie asked.

Ross grimaced. "I honestly don't know. Could be ten minutes. Could be an all-nighter."

"Tell you what," Callie said. "I'll hang out for a little bit. Then if you don't come back, I'll know it's an all-nighter, and I'll go on home. You call me when you're free again."

Ross stared at her. He released her, leaving wet finger-marks on her shirt, but he continued to scrutinize her and didn't back away.

"What?" she asked, hands going to her cheeks. "I have something on my face?"

"No. I'm wondering if you're real."

Callie touched her chest, her stomach, her hips. "Think so. Last time I checked, anyway."

Ross hauled her back to him. His next kiss was hard, opening her mouth, his arms tight around her. Callie hung in his grasp and enjoyed it until the kiss ended, leaving Callie shaking and hot.

"I will do my damnedest to make it the shortest meeting in River County history." Ross's voice was low, his eyes intense.

Callie believed him, but she'd lived with men who worked in time-consuming businesses all her life—her father with the ranch, Devon trying to claw his way to the top of his firm. Business came first, she'd learned. Relationships, second. Those in law enforcement were on call all the time to deal with anything from a rattlesnake in a house to drug dealers on a rampage.

"'Kay," she said.

Ross kissed her one more time, then he left the bathroom, grabbed a uniform from his walk-in closet, and had it on in two minutes. Callie stood back and watched him dress, Ross making it look like a dance.

One more kiss, then he was back downstairs. Ross unlocked his gun from a safe, holstered it, gave Callie yet another lingering kiss, and then was gone.

Callie watched from the front window as he strode through the dying evening light across the street toward the courthouse, leaping puddles as he went.

Her fingers on the blind's cord, Callie tried to decide how she felt, but nothing came to her clearly. Elation, disappointment, excitement, dizziness, uncertainty—all mixed into a dizzying swirl.

She concluded she shouldn't examine her emotions too closely. For now, she'd follow Ross's cue and take things as they came. See what happened. Not worry about making this a relationship.

And she absolutely, positively could not fall in love with him. That would be a complete disaster.

Now if she could make her pounding heart, tingling fingers, and very, very satisfied libido believe that.

ROSS KNEW RIGHT AWAY IT WASN'T GOING TO BE A SHORT meeting.

Hennessy, arms folded over his large chest, stood in front of all his deputies—four—and declared they were conducting a raid on the house in White Fork, almost certainly the temporary headquarters for one of the area's biggest dealers.

No one looked elated. They'd been keeping an eye on the house but didn't yet have a handle on how many people were involved or what kind of armament they had, mostly because Hennessy had said they shouldn't spare the manpower. Didn't want to give away the fact that they knew the dealers were there, he claimed.

"All right," Hennessy said now. "Let's roll."

Shawn McGregor, handsome, clean-cut, and Hennessy's

favorite, raised his hand. "Do we know what they're packing, sir?"

Good thing it was McGregor who'd asked the question. Hennessy would have snarled at any of the rest of them and told them to stop worrying like little girls. With McGregor, he'd actually answer.

"Nothing we can't handle. Remember, they think they're safe there. Let's show them they aren't."

Ross knew from experience that any suggestion that they summon backup, call a SWAT team, or alert the feds, would be dismissed. If any other agency complained about jurisdiction, Hennessy would say they'd simply acted on a tip to investigate suspicious activity, which was true. The sheriff was always good at covering his ass.

Hennessy usually stayed well out of the action, in any case, letting his deputies take the lead. He invoked his age as an excuse, claiming he'd be in the way of the younger deputies in a tight situation. He was better using his experience to direct, he'd say.

"Now, can we roll?" Hennessy asked impatiently. "I'd like to make these busts and get home to watch TV with my wife."

He would go home, he meant. The deputies would be stuck at the office doing the paperwork, which would be monumental if they arrested a houseful of suspected drug dealers. Ross and Sanchez exchanged a look but managed to keep their expressions neutral.

"You heard the boss," McGregor said. "Let's go."

Sanchez and Ross partnered, as usual. McGregor teamed up with a fairly new deputy, Joe Harrison, who'd arrived in Riverbend last year from San Antonio.

Ross had worried at first that a black deputy in a mostly white town would have a hard time, but so far, Joe had settled in with no problem—he was easygoing and quick with a smile, but he didn't take shit from anyone. The fact that Joe could get along with McGregor made him an extraordinary human being. Joe didn't toady to McGregor or pretend to like him, and he explained to Ross he was professional enough to suck it up and not let McGregor's attitude get in his way. Hennessy's either.

As Ross pulled his SUV from the lot, he couldn't help glancing up at his apartment window across the square. Sanchez, in the passenger seat, burst out laughing.

"Don't wave. You'll give it away."

Ross shot him a look, face burning. "What are you talking about?"

"I saw you and Callie go by, all cozy in her fancy car. And I didn't see her come out from your alley again. Don't worry, my friend. No one knows but me." Sanchez's laughter died to chuckles. "Lucky bastard."

Ross said nothing—didn't brag he'd had the most beautiful woman on earth in his bed. He didn't kiss and tell.

More mirth from Sanchez. "Man, the look on your face. Last thing you want to do tonight is bust up a bunch of smelly, well-armed dealers, am I right? Can't blame you."

"What the hell is Hennessy doing?" Ross asked, abruptly changing the subject. "We aren't ready to raid these guys. There might not be any evidence in there to hold them."

Sanchez shrugged. "He wants to go in hard, prove he's serving the community. He's up for reelection."

"Shit, is it that time already?"

Hennessy had been sheriff for years, so long that the election was more or less a formality. But during the months running up to the election, he made sure to be more visible, personally responding to calls or showing up at accident scenes to comfort victims and assure them that justice would be done.

"Means we're rushing into a scene where we could all get shot, so Hennessy can have some publicity, am I right?" Ross asked as he drove around the square, resolutely turning his face from his apartment's lighted windows.

"That's why we're wearing." Sanchez patted his bulletproof vest. "I'm thinking it's going to be a long night."

Ross tried to concentrate on driving as he entered the open highway that led to White Fork. The storm had passed, and the moon hung overhead, its light reflecting on the standing water on the pavement and ditches beyond.

Tried to concentrate. Ross's thoughts flitted to Callie, her body beneath his, the uninhibited way she'd cried out. She'd made love enthusiastically, no lying back and pretending to enjoy it while he got his rocks off. She'd wanted to be there, in his bed, having sex with him.

The fact that they'd made love in nothing but their socks for some reason heated Ross as he slid through the wet night. The humid air started to fog the windows—or maybe that was his thoughts of Callie.

A coyote rushed across the road. Ross braked and swerved, the SUV sliding on the wet pavement.

No one was around but them, McGregor's SUV far ahead, and Hennessy a long way behind. Ross dragged in a breath, straightened the SUV, and went on.

"Want me to drive?" Sanchez asked in a mild tone. "Seems like your heart isn't in it."

Yes, Ross should let him take the wheel. Hadn't occurred to him that he'd be distracted by thoughts of a woman—this had never happened to him before. Ross's passionate encounters rarely went much beyond a few times with any one woman. His irregular hours and sudden calls in to work—like tonight—was a turnoff.

Would it be for Callie? And why was he worried about that? He'd told her they'd keep it casual, take things as they came.

He was so full of shit. Ross wanted to latch on to her and never let her go.

"Yeah, I should be driving," Sanchez said decidedly. "You have your head up your ass, my friend."

"Sorry." Ross decided to go with humor. "Can't blame me, like you said. She's totally worth the head space."

"Great. You can double date with me and Sylvie. Ladies love the double date. Probably so they can gang up on us."

Sanchez and Sylvie Page had been going out forever, always together, never announcing a wedding date. If they'd lived together they'd be common-law married by now, but Sylvie had her own place a little way from town and owned a flower shop on the road that led to Lampasas. Sanchez lived in Riverbend on the opposite side of the square from Ross. Sylvie loved the guy but she said she slept better when she wasn't interrupted by his late-night calls. The relationship worked for them, and even the nosiest Riverbenders had stopped asking when they'd tie the knot.

They'd start asking Callie shit like that if she and Ross were seen together often enough. Callie would run for the hills.

"No double dating," Ross said firmly. "No dating at all. Keep it to yourself."

Sanchez looked surprised, but lifted his hands. "You got it. It's your life."

"And for fuck's sake, don't tell my brothers. I'd never hear the end of it."

"That's for sure. Like I said, don't worry. I got your back."

Which was why Ross had been friends with Sanchez for so long. Sanchez accepted and didn't judge.

Ross's brothers were very accepting too, but judged all the time. Even Carter, who was closest to Ross, would narrow his hazel eyes and ask what his intentions were.

"Thanks," Ross said. He and Sanchez rarely had to say *please* and *thank you,* but this was about Callie.

"Let's concentrate on surviving tonight. Then we'll talk."

Ross nodded. Hennessy had taken them into tight situations before, and only the deputies' experience and courage had got them out again. Made great headlines, but Ross preferred to keep his blood inside his body.

White Fork, a smaller town than Riverbend, was mostly residential and surrounded by farms. Kids spent the first eight years of school in White Fork, and then went to Riverbend for high school. Yellow school buses were a familiar sight on this highway.

The sidewalks rolled up here about nine. There was one roadhouse on the other side of town, far enough away that the noise and traffic didn't reach White Fork.

Lights were on in houses, most people at home and finishing up dinner. Ranchland lined the road even in the middle of town, and horses browsed in the fields beyond barbed wire fences.

The neighborhood the SUVs turned to—no lights or sirens —was a development built about thirty years ago, nice subur-ban-like dwellings for those who commuted to Austin or other big towns for white-collar jobs but liked living in the country. Simple but comfortable, the houses said. They were brick with white windows and black shutters, set on about a half acre each, plenty of space for the kids and dogs.

The house in question lay in the center of the development, and looked no different from the others. A few months ago, the house, which had been empty a while, had sold to a guy no one knew. Calls to the sheriff's office had started soon after that, neighbors reporting strange people coming and going at all hours, several cars parked in front for days that would then disappear, to be replaced with others they'd never seen before. The people of White Fork knew exactly what went on in their streets and weren't shy about telling.

Ross pulled over a few houses down from the target. McGregor and Joe Harrison were nowhere in sight. Neither was Hennessy, but Ross didn't worry. They each had their positions and would converge when Hennessy gave the signal.

"Dark in there," Ross said in a low voice. No lights shone in the windows, not even through slits in curtains or blinds. No cars were parked on the road and none stood in the driveway.

"Either they're lying very low, or this is a dead end," Sanchez said.

Ross didn't like this. Uneasiness tingled in his fingers, a signal he'd learned never to ignore.

He was reaching for his door handle when knuckles rapped on the window.

"Shit!" Ross peeled himself from the SUV's ceiling and quickly rolled down the window. "Manny?" he said in a harsh whisper to the shaking kid who stood outside his door. "What the hell are you doing here?"

Chapter Ten

✿❀✿

W arning you," Manny said breathlessly as Ross yanked open the door and climbed out to face him. "That house is empty. The dudes inside are long gone. They got a tip, and they hightailed it out of there."

The warm, humid evening wrapped Ross's body, and sweat trickled from his temples. "You've got ten seconds to tell me exactly how you know this."

Manny's face was pale in the moonlight. "Let me in the truck," he said frantically. "Please?"

Ross stared at him a moment then unlocked and opened the rear door. He shoved Manny in, slammed the door, and got himself back into the driver's seat.

"Hey, Deputy Sanchez," Manny said.

Sanchez lifted a hand to him, keeping his expression deadpan. "Manny."

Ross glared at Manny through the grill. "Ten seconds."

"Don't ask me," Manny said with a moan. "I got sources, okay? What I know is the dude who runs the house had a phone call. Next thing I know, he's telling his crew to disappear. Which they did. Don't ask me where, because I don't know."

Likely he didn't. Manny sometimes acted as lookout for criminal gangs, but they didn't trust him further than that. They'd ditch him as soon as they blew town and hire another lookout in their next base.

"In other words, they knew we were coming," Ross said.

"Looks like."

Sanchez blew out his breath. "Shit."

"How?" Ross demanded. They hadn't broadcast on the police frequency that they were heading up here. Mildred had rounded up Ross via the radio, yes, but a meeting at the sheriff's office could mean nothing more than a debate about the coffee fund, and the whole county knew it.

"It wasn't me," Manny said in a panic. "I didn't know anything until the boss got the phone call."

"Damn it." Ross picked up his radio and hailed McGregor. "They're gone," he said. "We missed them."

"What?" McGregor's surprised voice came back.

"You heard me."

"Copy." McGregor's disappointment drifted through the radio. He'd probably looked forward to being a hero.

"We should check out the house anyway," Ross added.

Fear filled Manny's voice. "No, Ross, don't go in there."

"Why not? You just said it was empty."

"What if they booby-trapped the place? What if they're lying in wait, guns ready?"

Always a possibility. But the dark house had an abandoned feel to it.

Sanchez answered. "It's why we go through all the training. Sit tight, kid. We'll be right out."

"No, no! Let me go." Manny banged on the door, which didn't open from the inside. "You can't arrest me. I haven't done anything."

"Would you calm down?" Ross got out and opened the

back door before Manny could bang again. "Get out, but stick close to the truck. And if any guys do rush from the house, run and hide. Don't get involved. It's not worth your life."

Manny gave him a scared look as he slithered from the back seat but nodded.

Ross settled his vest and checked that his gun was secure in its holster, and then he and Sanchez waited until McGregor and Harrison had pulled in on the other side of the house's driveway. McGregor wanted to go in the front—more glory, Ross supposed, so he and Sanchez slipped around back.

Ross drew his pistol and made sure a bullet was in the chamber before he moved quietly forward, sticking to shadows and avoiding the windows. No shades or curtains blocked the windows facing the backyard, and through them, Ross saw an airy house with a few pieces of furniture in it.

The back door was unlocked. Ross walked right in just as McGregor had Harrison bash in the front door. Ross kept out of the line of fire in case McGregor decided to shoot at anything that moved.

The living room was silent and deserted. Ross, Sanchez, and Harrison searched room to room, while McGregor waited by the front door. Nobody was there.

They found no evidence of drug dealing either. No handy bags of cocaine, blocks of heroin, or jars of meth. Not even a baggy of weed ready to be rolled.

The inhabitants had left no clothing, razors, or even tooth-brushes in the bathroom, no laundry in the hampers or the clothes washer. There were dishes in the dishwasher, washed, the "sanitized" light on. The dishes weren't distinctive—they could be purchased at the local big box store.

Ross heard Hennessy's outraged tones through McGregor's radio. He ordered the deputies to scour every inch of the house. "You enjoy yourselves," Hennessy snapped. "I'm going home."

"You heard him," McGregor said after he clicked off his radio. "Every inch."

"McGregor, you don't outrank me," Sanchez said in annoyance.

"So?" McGregor's light brown eyes widened. "Doesn't mean we shouldn't obey his orders."

"I know," Sanchez growled. "I'm just pointing it out."

Harrison and Ross exchanged a look, and Ross barely kept his eyes from rolling. McGregor had the habit of trying to take over every mission.

They went over the house with great care but found nothing. That is, until Harrison discovered a cell phone, one of the old style flip phones Ross was surprised still existed.

Harrison held it up in his plastic gloved hands, and McGregor quickly stepped forward with a paper evidence bag. "Put that right in here."

He was going to take credit for it, Ross thought in disgust. "Good work, Harrison," he said. "You must have missed that, McGregor."

McGregor curled his lip. "You're adorable, Campbell. I'll let Harrison engrave his name on it if you want."

Harrison dropped the phone into the bag without changing expression—he'd worked in a large county with a big sheriff's department and must have heard ten times the bickering there.

"Well, that's it," McGregor said, folding up the bag. "There's fuck-all here. I bet no one was ever here, and our intel was bad."

"Happens," Sanchez said. "At least the paperwork will be easy. One house, empty except for one cell phone. Sign and date, and I go home tonight. I bet we all have something to get back to." He made sure the others couldn't see his wink at Ross.

Ross didn't give him the satisfaction of responding.

He glanced around the living room one last time before he

walked out via the front door, looking forward to ditching the vest, which was close in the July heat.

"They were here, Ross, I swear to God."

Manny materialized from a shadow near the house, and Ross smothered a shout of surprise.

"Manny, what the hell part of *wait by the truck* did you not understand?"

"No one's here," Manny argued. "Like I said. But they were. A big cowboy and a bunch of losers. I don't know where they went. Their distributors would drive up and take the stuff, leaving the money."

Ross had pretty much known that from surveillance, though they'd never caught anyone in the act of exchanging, nor had anyone who'd been stopped and searched revealed a thing. These guys knew how to cover their tracks.

"I'm not usually a narc." Manny folded his arms. "But they were assholes."

"Stiffed you, did they?" Sanchez asked from behind Ross.

Manny looked chagrined. "Yeah, they did."

Ross stopped Manny with an intense look. "No, you mean, *you have no idea what Sanchez is talking about.*"

Manny looked startled, then his eyes widened, and he nodded. "I have no idea what you're talking about, Deputy Sanchez."

"You just happened to be taking a walk and noticed these guys in the house."

"Yep. That's what I did."

Ross gave him a nod. "That's what I thought. Come on. I'll drive you home."

When he was off duty, he'd grill Manny more about the phone call, but for now, Ross wanted to finish this wasted night and see if he could make it to his apartment before Callie left.

Sanchez rode with them, glum and silent. Back in River-bend, Ross dropped Manny at the line of trailers that skirted an inlet from the river. Manny insisted on being left at the end of the road, and he jogged off into the darkness. At least he went the direction of the trailer where he lived with his dad.

Ross and Sanchez didn't say much on the way to the station, Sanchez only stating, "Sucks that you ruined your date night for nothing."

Ross could only agree.

He tried not to hurry as he wrote up his report and then signed out and walked around the square and across the street to his apartment. The windows were dark, as he figured they would be.

Callie's car wasn't in his garage when he let himself in the back way. He'd known she'd be gone, but his heart sank as he climbed the stairs.

The apartment felt doubly empty now that Callie had been in it. Ross locked up his gun, the process automatic. He unbuttoned his shirt and moved to the kitchen, bypassing the coffeemaker for the refrigerator and a beer.

As he twisted the cap from the bottle, he found a paper towel spread out on the counter. The mug Callie had drunk from rested on it, clean. A pen lay next to the paper towel, and with it, she'd written:

Thanks for the coffee.

Callie.

She'd drawn a little heart by her name.

Ross folded the note carefully and carried it across the room to the drawer in the side table where he kept his most treasured keepsakes. There wasn't much—a pearl-handled jackknife that had belonged to his father, a ribbon he'd won for marksmanship, photos of himself and his brothers from a stunt show they'd done as kids.

Callie's note nestled among them now. Ross closed the drawer and snapped off the light.

CALLIE ENTERED THE OFFICE OF AGCT ENTERPRISES ON the opposite side of the square from Ross's apartment the next morning, keeping a ten o'clock appointment with Karen Marvin.

A receptionist, the younger sister of a girl Callie had known in school, greeted her in a small but pristine foyer softened with potted plants and a gigantic fresh-flower arrangement. Changing that every day or so probably kept the town's one florist's shop in business.

Though Callie had only met Karen in passing, she'd heard much about her. Karen, originally from California, had come to Riverbend, during the time Callie had been living in Dallas, to help her ex-husband's Houston development company buy up land. But Karen had quickly fallen in love with Riverbend and decided instead to assist locals, with the aid of the Campbells, to fend off developers by helping them pay their mortgages or build up small businesses. That she'd destroyed her ex-husband's plans to turn Riverbend into a cookie-cutter suburban community in the process had been a bonus.

Karen's office was a mix of big-city sleekness softened by small-town touches, like a polished wood desk and bookcases similar to the ones in Ross's apartment.

Karen held out a slim hand to shake, a diamond bracelet winking on her wrist. She wore a pale linen suit against the heat and had her blond hair in a French braid. Her smile was businesslike tinged with warmth.

"How are you?" she asked, her accent that of a transplant from another state who'd picked up a slight drawl. "Ross has told me all about you." She squeezed Callie's hand before she released it. "The Campbell boys sure are hot, aren't they?"

Callie raised her brows. She agreed, but it wasn't what she'd expected the manager of a charity to say.

"Don't mind my frankness, honey," Karen said, waving her to a seat. "I see no need to hide the truth about men. Those Campbells are gorgeous, and you know it."

"Well, yes." Callie flashed a smile and sat, nervous about her upcoming spiel. She wasn't certain where to begin.

A hard knock sounded on the door, and Tyler Campbell entered. "Hey, Callie," he said. "I asked Karen if I could sit in. I want to know all about this ranch idea."

Tyler, a year older than Callie, had been considered the wildest Campbell. Right after high school his longtime girl-friend had been killed, and he'd gone through a series of short-term affairs, gaining him the reputation as a skirt chaser. Callie had figured that much of his recklessness with women came from grief.

Recently, he'd married a young woman from Dallas who'd already had a kid, and now Jess was expecting Tyler's child, any day now. The change in Tyler was amazing—the wildness had turned into a deep happiness, Callie could see from his warm smile and calm gaze.

Tyler, whose easygoing ways appealed to everyone, did the PR work for the Circle C training ranch and kept happy those hiring the brothers as stunt riders. Callie understood from his mother that Tyler now did the same for AGCT Enterprises, their new nonprofit.

Callie felt shy outlining her dream, but Tyler's interested questions put her at her ease. She had to admire the teamwork —Karen all business, Tyler all charm.

She handed them the folder she'd put together when she and Nicole had agreed on the idea to move the rehab ranch to Riverbend. Expenses, income, funding from charitable organi-zations and fundraisers, employees, volunteers, the horses' needs, insurance, and a host of other details.

"I talked with Dr. Anna, the vet my father uses, and she's willing to donate some hours and supplies," Callie finished. "She thinks it's a great idea."

"Yeah, we know Anna," Tyler said. "You can't have horses around here and *not* know her. Glad she's on board."

Karen cleared her throat, the sound deflating Callie's opti-

mism. Tyler was the enthusiasm, she decided, Karen the prac-
tical side.

"Animals are notoriously costly," Karen said. "And you're
talking about horses that will need a lot of medical attention,
not to mention feed. Have you considered the reality of the
expense? Of the work?"

"Yes." Callie answered without hesitation, sure of her
ground. "I've taken care of horses all my life—cows too, by the
way. I've helped bring in foals and set a horse's leg. I can dose
them, get them on their feet, walk them, trailer them ... you
name it. I'll be working just as hard as Nicole and the volunteers. We figure we'll need a couple of paid employees for
bookkeeping and stable management, then volunteers who love
horses to care for them and find them homes."

"Well, I think you're a little crazy," Karen said, "though I
like the idea. Tyler tells me your father is one of the best busi-
nessmen in cattle ranching. I admit I don't know a lot about it,
but I figure if he hasn't gone broke, he must know what he's
doing. He'll back you?"

"He's said so, yes. My dad likes a profit, but he also enjoys
helping people—and horses."

The three of them were being so polite. Callie refrained
from crossing her fingers. Tyler could smile all he wanted, but
Callie had the feeling that if Karen said no, that would be it.

Tyler's cell phone jangled, and he gave them an apologetic
look. "Sorry." He frowned at the readout then turned his back
and answered. "Ross? What's up?"

Callie couldn't hide her start. The previous night flooded
back to her—Ross's warmth on top of her, their bare bodies
sliding together, his kisses on her skin. Ross smiling at her in
the dark, touching her with slow fingers.

The sight of him coming out of the shower, naked and dripping, had imprinted itself on her brain and wouldn't go away.

Karen noticed Callie's sudden flush, and the woman's coral-
shaded lips quirked.

Tyler turned around, his face gray. Karen's amusement turned to concern. "Tyler, you all right?"

Callie rose. "Is it your wife?"

Tyler nodded numbly. He opened his mouth to speak then closed it again.

"Tyler?" Ross's voice came over the phone. *"You still there?"*

Tyler continued to stand wordlessly, and Callie went quickly to him and took the phone.

"Ross? It's Callie. What's wrong?"

"Nothing's wrong. Unless you count Jess's water breaking in the kitchen, and Grace running around like crazy, and Faith and Dominic squealing until my eardrums are ready to pop. I'm taking Jess to the clinic. Tell Tyler to meet us there. *If* you can make him understand you."

Callie glanced at Tyler, who looked poleaxed. Karen had leapt to her feet and was trying to shove a steaming coffee cup at him. Tyler only stared at it as though he'd never seen coffee before.

"I'd better drive him," Callie said. "I don't think he can move on his own."

"That'd be great, sweetheart." Ross's voice rumbled over her with pleasant fieriness.

He clicked off, and Callie handed the phone back to Tyler.

"Come on," she said, excitement brimming. "Your wife's having a baby."

Chapter Eleven

J ess told Ross in no uncertain terms that he was *not* to draw attention as he drove her to the clinic at the crossroads between Riverbend and White Fork, where everyone in the county had their babies.

Ross grinned at her, turned on his lights and sirens, and sped out of town.

"It's an emergency," he said as Jess glared at him, hand on her belly. "Can't have Tyler's kid popping out in my SUV."

"I'll get you for this." Jess sent him a mock scowl.

Ross, for his speed, drove carefully. Cars and trucks pulled over when they saw his lights.

A silver Mercedes moved competently to the side of the road to let them pass. Ross glimpsed Callie's beautiful face in the driver's side window and the dark bulk of someone in the passenger seat. Must be Tyler. Ross flashed his headlights as he glided past, and Callie pulled in behind him.

Ross reached the clinic well ahead of them, swooping up the driveway to deposit Jess at the ER. An orderly came out with a wheelchair, and Ross dashed to the passenger side to help Jess down. She sent him a grateful look, her eyes shining with both excitement and worry.

Callie's car halted behind Ross's SUV, and Tyler staggered out. "Jess!"

Jess turned to him, and the joy on her face made Ross's eyes sting. When had he turned into such a sap?

Tyler helped Jess into the wheelchair, and the orderly pushed her inside, Tyler holding her hand all the way.

Ross sensed Callie approach, and then she was beside him, her cool voice a balm in the hot morning. "Good," she said. "They made it. I'm glad they'll be together."

"Me too. Though Jess is going to kill me for the sirens." He chuckled. "She'll get over it."

"I thought Tyler would pass out. He's terrified." They watched Jess and Tyler disappear, the two clinging to each other. "Poor guy."

"He'll get over that too," Ross said. "Or—maybe not. Taking care of a newborn won't be a picnic."

"Not much sleeping for him, I guess."

They shared a look, Callie's smile making her eyes sparkle.

Just like that, Ross knew, in one moment, what he wanted in his life.

Callie glanced around, breaking the spell. "I need to move my car. This is a loading zone."

Absolutely no one was rushing to load or unload anyone, but security would probably come out to tell them to clear the driveway. Callie turned away.

"Wait," Ross said. He liked how quickly she swung back to him. "You want to get something to eat? The cafeteria is kind of crappy, but—"

"Sure," Callie said before he could finish. "I have the feeling my appointment with AGCT has been postponed."

Flashing another smile, she darted to her car and drove it smoothly to the parking lot.

CALLIE MET ROSS OUTSIDE THE CAFETERIA, WHICH HAD JUST finished its breakfast service and hadn't started lunch, but they grabbed iced teas and plastic-wrapped muffins from its front counter and took a table near the window.

"Jess is settling in, Tyler told me," Ross said. "It will be a while, though. I figure I'll leave them alone for now. We'll call everyone in when it's time."

Callie wasn't certain she should be there when the rest of the family arrived for the birth, but at the moment, it was nice to face Ross across the table. He wore his uniform, but he explained his shift didn't start until that evening—he'd be at the station most of the night.

"Life of a cop," he said, shrugging.

Callie wasn't certain how to respond. He'd said they should take things as they came, but she had no experience with being casual. Her expected role with Devon had been spelled out for her—*supportive girlfriend, never be demanding, hang out with your own friends until I'm ready for you.*

She'd never sat in a hospital cafeteria and just talked to a man. Men and women, Devon had implied, weren't supposed to be *friends.* Guys before that had mostly thought the same.

Ross apparently hadn't received the memo. He rested one arm easily on the table while he took uninhibited sips of tea through his straw around snacking on the packaged muffin.

"Stuff's kind of rank," he said, studying the label. "Maybe Grace should give up on the pastry shop idea and cater the clinic."

"I thought she was planning to open a restaurant in Fredericksburg," Callie said.

"She was, but her business partner ran out on her with the money. She's been selling her pastries through the diner and is saving up to open a bakery on the square. But then Zach came along, and now she's a little busy." He finished with a laugh.

Zach was Grace and Carter's nearly year-old son. Grace and Carter were also raising Faith, Carter's daughter. Callie at least knew that much.

"I'm out of the Riverbend loop," she said regretfully. "Too much time in Dallas and then hiding out at the ranch. Our housekeeper gives me some of the news, but she doesn't believe in talking about people behind their backs, darn it."

"She must be the only one in River County who thinks like that." Ross crumpled the empty plastic and pushed it aside. "Let me catch you up on the dirt."

He launched into tales of his brothers, while Callie nibbled her stale muffin, how Adam the movie stuntman had returned to training horses, occasionally taking a movie job, but as stunt coordinator, riding stunts only if he wanted to. Mostly, though, he and Bailey stayed in their new house not far from the ranch and enjoyed their son Dale. They hadn't said anything, but Ross suspected another Campbell baby would be coming along next year.

Grant and Christina were living in the shotgun house with their little girl, Grant as full of himself as ever. But Ross was glad for him, because he and Christina had been through some rough times.

Tyler and Jess had built a house on the other side of the ranch, which they'd just moved into. Ross and his brothers had been recruited for the heavy lifting.

Ross then turned to his friends and neighbors, talking about how the Malorys had become closer friends since Carter and Grace had married. He told Callie how Karen Marvin had a new cowboy on her arm every month, and people joked she was collecting them for a calendar. But they respected her acumen and acknowledged how much she'd helped the people of Riverbend.

As he spoke, Callie relaxed. This man loved his family, as much as he grumbled about them, and enjoyed the people in their small town. Callie came from a close family too and understood the mixture of love and exasperation.

She found herself opening up, telling him about Evelyn, who had a beautiful voice, and was knocking the socks off of the music crowd in Austin. Callie wasn't sure how far her career would go—local girl made good or superstardom—but Evelyn was happy.

Her other sister, Montana, was struggling through the male-dominated field of astronomy. She was smart, had her PhD, and deserved recognition for her work on supernovas.

"I'm not exactly sure what she does," Callie admitted. "I went to her lab once, and she mostly stares at rows of numbers, which made no sense to me." She shook her head. "But she's a good teacher. I sat in on her class, and she had her students laughing and asking all kinds of questions. In my science classes it was always the professor talking a mile a minute while we scrambled to take notes in dead silence."

"Yeah, I had teachers like that in college," Ross said. "I went for a criminal justice degree. I'd already been hired on as a deputy, because this county is always desperate for people, but I wanted the degree so I wouldn't remain at the bottom of the ranks. Not that it's helped me. Hennessy has his own agenda."

He took an immediate sip of tea as though regretting speaking the sheriff's name. Ross had done that in his apartment, too, when she'd joked that the county's criminals weren't used to honest cops.

Callie was good at putting two and two together, and she wondered what Ross didn't want to say about Sheriff Hennessy.

Callie's father didn't like the man much and had backed the few who'd dared run against him in the past. Most people had given up getting Hennessy out of office—he'd be in his seat until he dropped over, was common consensus.

"You should run for sheriff," Callie said on impulse.

Ross took his straw out of his mouth to laugh. He had a smooth laugh, which warmed the air. "You're funny."

"Why not?" Callie's zeal grew. "Everyone likes you, you're good at your job, and you're a Campbell, which gives you a lot of clout. One of the oldest and most respected families in the county."

"So are the Joneses. Why don't you run?"

Callie poked her ice with her straw. "Sure, Ross. I think the population would head for the hills if there was a chance a woman would become sheriff. I love Riverbend, but it's a seriously old-fashioned town. Women really run the county, but the guys have to pretend they do."

"That's for sure." Ross didn't look offended. "Hennessy would wipe the floor with my ass if I decided to run against him. Or send guys to do it for him."

He shrugged off her suggestion, but Callie saw a spark in his eyes, as though the idea had taken hold.

A county sheriff would have even less time to explore a budding relationship, she knew. Was she trying to put obstacles between them? And why?

Fear, she realized. Pure and simple. Callie had walked out of fire after Devon, and she feared being burned again.

Ross was smart to say they should take things as they came. Because maybe nothing would come after all.

Callie studied his strong fingers around his cup, remembering the gentleness of them on her body. She had a hard time breathing correctly around him.

She could go for enjoying his presence, his touch, listening to his deep voice as he talked, laughed. She'd learn how to savor every moment together, and not worry about the end.

Take it slow. Callie wouldn't mind that, if *slow* meant getting to know each other over the next ten years.

Callie didn't realize how much time had passed until Grace and Carter arrived with Faith and Dominic, Jess's son from her first marriage. Dominic looked worried, though Grace was trying to keep his spirits up.

Grant and Christina entered behind them. No babies with either couple, but Callie figured they'd not want to bring them to the clinic.

Bailey and Adam, it turned out, had volunteered to be the designated baby watchers while the others and Olivia came to see the wild Tyler Campbell become a father.

"I should go," Callie said quietly to Ross.

They'd been in the cafeteria for hours, lunch having come and gone, talking about everything and nothing. It had been a long time since Callie had *talked* to anyone who actually listened. Even her sisters, as close as they were, had their own lives, their own troubles. She hadn't realized how much she'd needed this connection.

"Why?" Ross gave her a puzzled look as they joined his family. "You all remember Callie."

Christina was Montana's age, and had been what Callie and her friends called one of the "older girls," at school, and so the object of veneration. Christina and Montana had graduated five years before Callie.

Callie was closer in age to Grace, who had been two grades ahead of her. Grace Malory had always been super-sweet, a debutante herself, and had given Callie lots of guidance. Grace also had two hunk-a-licious brothers the female population of Riverbend wanted to get close to. Result—Grace had a lot of friends.

Grace brightened when she saw Callie and immediately hugged her. "So good to see you," she said in true gladness. Grace did not have a false bone in her. Callie hugged her hard, her shyness falling away.

"How you doing, Callie?" Christina asked, a touch more formally.

Callie put on her warmest smile. "I'm just fine. I hear you have a beautiful baby girl. Congratulations."

Christina softened, and Grant's pride took over his expression. "She's the most gorgeous thing I ever did see," Grant boomed. "Her mama excepted."

Christina's happiness radiated from her as she turned to Grant. These two were so much in love, it was palpable. It gave Callie a wistful feeling.

The family gathered, the three brothers towering over the ladies. Dominic still worried about his mother, so Callie offered to buy him and Faith an ice cream.

"You're pretty," Dominic said as Callie got them both soft-serve cones and paid at the register. "Are you going to marry Uncle Ross?"

Callie jumped, a drop of chocolate ice cream staining her pristine interview-day slacks.

Faith, nearly twelve if Callie remembered right, and starting to grow tall, grinned. "That would be awesome. Uncle Ross is lonely."

Callie glanced quickly across the room where Ross talked animatedly with his family. Carter had his arm around Grace, and Christina snuggled into Grant. Callie hoped no one had heard.

Ross did stand out among them, his crisp uniform contrasting the jeans, T-shirts, and cowboy boots of his brothers. Carter and Grant had calmed way down from when Callie had seen them last—spending a few years out of town gave her fresh perspective, and the change in the Campbell brothers was remarkable. Their lives had been stabilized by the women in their embraces, as well as the children here and waiting for them at home. Marriage hadn't exactly "tamed" them, Callie could see, but they were no longer reckless, searching.

Ross stood apart from them, not only because of his uniform, but because observant Faith was right—he was alone.

He had that alert and restless look of someone who wasn't hankering to rush home.

Callie led the kids with their ice cream back to the group. Ross gave her a look of gratitude that warmed her to her toes.

Olivia burst in through the door. Her tanned face was flushed, her eyes sparkling with gladness.

"She's here. Miss Sarah Campbell, seven pounds, five ounces."

Grant whooped, and Ross echoed him. Dominic imitated them, his yell robust. Carter, always quiet, cracked a smile, and Grace and Faith shared an excited hug.

"Can we see her?" Christina asked.

"Is my mom all right?" Dominic demanded at the same time. Callie put her arm around him, never minding his ice cream that led to the further ruin of her pants. He was the only one truly scared, she understood. Having his mom be rushed to the hospital had probably terrified him.

"She's wonderful, honey," Olivia assured him. "She did amazing, and she's asking for you."

She held out her hand, and Dominic, after giving Callie's a squeeze, ran to her. Olivia led him away, Faith skipping after them, the others pouring behind them.

Callie hung back. This was a family thing, and she wasn't part of the family. She'd depart and leave them with their joy.

Her heart sank at the thought of going back to her own house, big and empty with her folks gone. Maybe she'd drive into Austin, do some shopping, have a spa day, pamper herself. Go over her business plan again and reschedule with Karen Marvin.

Ross had gone out the swinging door of the cafeteria, leaving Callie alone with the cooks who were prepping dinner.

The door swung one way, and when it swung back, Ross came with it. "Come on. They move fast, but we'll catch up."

Callie took up her purse. "I really need to go. Things to do."

"What things? Don't let them scare you away. They're just Campbells."

He held out his large and strong hand, his look welcoming.

Callie hesitated. Running off would be rude to Ross. Staying—which she really wanted to—would be butting in on the rest of them. Tough choice.

Maybe not so tough. She'd never seen anyone more handsome than Ross as he reached out to her and smiled in excitement. Only watching his face over hers in the comfort of his bed had been better.

"Guess I can stay a while," she said. She took his hand, her blood warming as his smile deepened, and he led her out.

SARAH OLIVIA CAMPBELL WAS TINY, BLACK-HAIRED, AND scowling, and endeared herself immediately to the family that trooped in to see her.

Ross watched his brother Tyler transform as he held the tiny bundle in his arms, his face quiet with wonder. Jess, who looked gorgeous for a woman who'd just gone through labor and childbirth, gazed at Tyler with love.

Ross felt Callie's fingers twine around his. Her eyes shone with tears as she watched the magic of a family coming together.

Dominic hung back a little, as though worried he'd hurt his mom or the new baby, but Jess opened her arms and gathered him up. "Missed you, sweetie," she said, dropping a kiss to his unruly hair.

Dominic relaxed against her then popped up to examine the little sister Tyler crouched down to show him. Dominic peered at her tiny face, and a protective look came over him.

"Can I teach her to ride a motorcycle?" he asked.

"And a horse," Faith said quickly. "She'll be winning ribbons in no time." Faith had a wall filled with her own.

"Give her a chance to decide," Ross said. "She might want to ice skate instead."

Faith and Dominic looked at Ross as though he'd lost his mind. He wished he could snap a picture of their faces.

"All right, time to go," Ross said. Jess, though happy, was drooping, and Tyler was giving Ross the eye. Four was company, everyone else, a crowd. "Nothing more to see here, folks. Move along."

He swept out the family, Faith still dancing. "I have so many cousins now," she said happily. "And I'm the oldest. This is great."

Somehow all the Campbells and Sullivans got out of the room, down the elevator, and out of the clinic to the parking lot. Somehow, Callie was with Ross all the way.

"I really do have to go," Callie said softly as they emerged into the late afternoon sunshine. "I need to call Karen and make sure I didn't blow my chance by not going back to the meeting."

"Karen understands. She'll blame Tyler. Bet he couldn't stand up when he got the news. You were nice to drive him."

"I was doing the community a favor." Callie's impish look catapulted Ross back to the night before, when she'd smiled at him across his pillow. Damn, he needed to see her there again. "Keeping a dangerous driver off the road."

"Well, it was sweet of you." Ross paused at her car, which she'd parked not far from the door. His sheriff's SUV was a few spaces down. "Thanks."

He leaned down and gently kissed her. Callie's mouth softened under his, and she touched his face.

Ross's body ignited. If they hadn't been in a public parking lot, he in uniform, his brothers and sisters-in-law and niece looking on interestedly, he'd scoop her up to him and turn this kiss into something more promising.

As it was, he brushed another kiss to her lips and eased back.

"See you soon," he said, tying not to sound too desperate.

"Breakfast?" Callie asked. "When you come off your shift? If you're still awake, that is."

"Perfect." Ross couldn't resist kissing her again.

Callie returned the kiss, touched his cheek one more time, and then got into her sleek, rich-girl car and started the engine. The smile she gave him as she pulled out, her car purring, made him want to leap into the air and whoop like Manny sometimes did, but Ross maintained his dignity and gave her a friendly wave.

He watched until she was well down the highway then turned to his own truck.

To find his brothers Grant and Carter standing before him like a wall, the scowls on their faces not boding anything good.

Chapter Twelve

R oss hadn't been intimidated by his older brothers since before he could walk. They'd been his protectors, his babysitters, the cool guys who'd taught him to ride horses and fight and woo ladies. He'd tried to emulate them, but also watched their mistakes and learned from them.

Carter, when he'd come along, had been uncomfortable with Grant and Adam and tried to compete with the two oldest boys for his place. Ross, the observer, had sensed Carter needed to be needed.

Ross had started asking Carter for help, seeking his advice about bullies in school, or asking for his protection, when the truth was that Ross could charm his way out of any situation. Carter had responded to Ross, becoming his older brother in truth. Carter had continued his rivalry with Adam and Grant and even the easygoing Tyler, but he'd confided in Ross many things he'd have never told the others.

Now Carter was giving him a cold stare. Ross faced two granite-hard faces and two pairs of angry eyes, Grant's blue, Carter's hazel.

"What's up?" Ross asked. "I gotta get to work."

He gave them his little-brother grin, the one that had always turned these big, mean cowboys into mush.

"Callie Jones," Carter said, not moving.

Ross was good at not losing his temper, but anger touched him. "Yeah, that was Callie Jones. You were standing right there when I introduced her."

"What he means is, what's going on with you two?" Grant asked in his low rumble. "I was joking around at the barbecue, but then you left with her, I hear she was at your apartment until late last night, and now you bring her to see Jess and Tyler's baby—"

"She gave Tyler a ride from Karen's office," Ross interrupted, his irritation growing. "Tyler couldn't walk, let alone drive. I wasn't going to tell Callie to get lost after she'd been so nice. If anything, we owe her gas money."

"Don't talk around the question," Grant said. "You always do that—makes me batshit crazy."

"What Grant means," Carter cut over him in a slow drawl, "is that she's not the kind of woman you have a fling with and dump. It's all over town she's sleeping with you now, and they're saying it started when you picked her up on her wedding day. Gossip like that pisses me off, but you need to know."

"Plus, if you break up with her, you're going to be reviled all over the county," Grant warned. "Won't matter if she's the one who walks out on *you*. The Jones sisters are princesses, high on a pedestal. Everyone likes you, Ross, but when it comes to taking sides between a Campbell and a Jones, I'm telling you, you'll lose. If you ease back now, they won't punish you too much."

Ross stared at the both of them. "Let me get this straight. You think I'm planning to use Callie for fun and walk away from her? And the county will never forgive me if I do?"

Grant scowled all the more. "You get away with a lot, baby bro, but if you hurt Callie, the town will give *you* as much hell as they give the rest of us. Plus they'll come down on us for letting you touch her."

Ross ran a hand through his hair, his jaw tightening. "First of all, I think I know more about opinion in this county than y'all do—I'm out in it every day, talking to people while you're holed up at the ranch. Second, why are so quick to think I'm not getting serious with Callie, that I'm going to dump her?"

"Because it's what you do," Grant pointed out. "You see a lady you like, have a fling, walk away."

"By mutual agreement," Ross returned in a hard voice. "Usually it's because once she figures out what crappy hours I keep, she takes off for someone who can pay more attention to her. I'm rarely the one doing the dumping."

Ross had learned, painfully, that women wanted the danger and romance of dating a cop but not the tedious reality. After he stood them up a time or two because he had to break up a fight or write an endless report or sit through one of Hennessy's mandatory meetings, they said good-bye. He'd taught himself to keep things casual, which decreased the disappointment when the brief relationship ended.

He'd looked at Callie today across the table in the cafeteria, and knew it had already gone far beyond casual, at least on his side. When she walked away, the crush of it would take a long, long time to fade.

"Do me a favor," Ross said in clipped tones. "Don't talk about me and Callie. You have no idea what's between us, and to be blunt, it's none of your business. Now I have something to tell you—I'm thinking about running for sheriff. Think you can back off me once I can send your asses to jail?"

Grant blinked, and now Carter frowned. Carter had never had the best relationship with law enforcement, though he'd come to terms with Ross being a deputy, understanding that Ross wanted to help people, not constrict them.

"You can already send us to jail," Grant pointed out. "You'd run against Hennessy? Are you nuts? He has every election tied up."

"I wasn't saying I'd win," Ross said. "But Hennessy needs to be shaken up a little. People are tired of him. I could at least make him work to get votes instead of assume he's cinched it. Might make him clean up his act."

"He'll fire your ass," Carter warned. "Win or lose."

Ross shrugged. "Maybe. But he shouldn't get away with anything he wants because no one's brave enough to stand up to him."

"You'd have to move out of the county, maybe even the state," Grant said, the lightness in his voice forced. "That would be a shame. We'd miss you."

"You keep telling me the town loves me, or at least they will unless I dump Callie," Ross said, ideas beginning to coalesce.

"Partly because her dad owns half the county," Grant said. "Money talks."

"Exactly. Callie's dad has nothing good to say about Sheriff Hennessy. If I can convince him to support me—the town might just pick the Joneses *and* the Campbells."

While Carter looked thoughtful, Grant's face darkened. "You better not be thinking about using Callie to make yourself sheriff. I'd have to kick your ass."

Ross gave him an outraged look. "I'll kick *your* ass for thinking I'd do that. I'll leave my relationship with Callie totally out of it—you just made me remember how much her dad doesn't like Hennessy. Anyway, me running for sheriff was her idea. It had been in the back of my mind, but she's the first person who said it out loud."

And when Callie voiced it, Ross *believed*.

Carter's thoughtfulness turned to sharp scrutiny, then he gave Ross a slow nod of understanding.

"If you decide to run, I'm there for you," Carter said. "Let me know what I can do."

Grant started to laugh. "Damn, bro, you have balls. I'd love to see Hennessy taken down a peg, so I'm with you too." He clapped Ross on the shoulder. "How awesome is that? Our little brother's going to be sheriff of River County."

———————

KAREN AGREED TO RESCHEDULE CALLIE'S APPOINTMENT, saying she could be bribed with pictures of Jess and Tyler's baby. Callie hadn't taken photos herself, so she texted Olivia, who sent her a deluge. The best one was of Tyler and Jess with heads bent over Sarah, Dominic on tiptoe to look at his sister.

Result—Callie's appointment was at three the next afternoon.

That morning, Callie and Ross met for breakfast as arranged, at the diner, of course. Callie could tell he was tired after his all-night shift, his eyes red-rimmed, but he ate a hearty breakfast and talked animatedly. Admittedly, he drank lots of coffee.

Callie hoped he'd suggest she walk him home, but Ross, after holding a shaking hand over his coffee cup to prevent a refill, said, "I have to be back at work at noon. Just enough time to shower and crash for a few hours."

Her eyes widened. "That's a crazy schedule."

He shrugged, his weariness evident. "It is what it is. There's only four deputies, so we rotate a lot. A shorter shift today, though. Off at seven."

Callie could tell he was holding back yawns, so she said she'd talk to him later, pretending she wouldn't miss him all day.

Ross left without kissing her in front of the interested patrons, but he did give her hand a hard squeeze under the table before he went. He exchanged greetings with his friends and acquaintances on his way out, never mind matter how tired he was. Everyone liked Ross.

He'd also paid for her breakfast, Callie discovered when

she went to the register. Mrs. Ward offered no opinion about it, but she didn't hide the twinkle in her eyes.

Callie went home, put on jeans and boots and headed for Anna Lawler's place.

Dr. Anna, as everyone called her, had moved back to Riverbend from San Angelo a year ago. She'd grown up in Riverbend but left to go to vet school and then had been taken on by a large-animal vet in San Angelo. When the veterinarian in Riverbend retired, Anna had jumped at the chance to move home and take over the practice.

Callie had been friends with Anna growing up, and was delighted to see her back.

Anna had been the shy girl, bookish and awkward, preferring to read or be with horses and dogs instead of people. Callie, who'd been secretly shy but had learned to hide it, had bonded with her. The socialite and the bookworm had formed an unusual friendship.

Now Anna, just under five feet tall, her blond hair worn in a tight braid, her eyes cornflower blue, had to fight a battle of a different kind—to convince the ranchers, farmers, and cowboys of River County that she could treat their animals just fine.

She did it by never raising her voice, but she also never backed down. Callie had watched her one day at the Jones ranch, when the cowboys hadn't wanted to let her vaccinate part of the herd, saying no lady could handle the unruly cattle.

Anna had calmly handed the biggest, toughest ranch hand a syringe and said, "Go ahead. Grab that bull and jab him."

The bull in question, kept for breeding purposes, had already been put into a pen, but he'd been steaming mad about it. He'd torn around the small corral, slamming his horned head into its wooden poles. The fencing groaned and bent whenever he hit it.

The cowboy had paled and hung back.

Anna had climbed the fence, caught the bull and bent his

head down, poked the needle into the fleshy folds in his neck, patted him, and opened the gate to let him out into the pasture.

The Jones cowboys hadn't given her any shit after that.

Today Anna was finishing up a shoeing job—she also assisted the farrier when there was a lot of work.

She gave the shoe a few more taps with her hammer, released the strap that held the horse's foot, and stroked the horse's side, telling him he'd been a good boy.

"What's up, Callie?" she asked, leaving the horse to be led back to its trailer. "I heard Tyler Campbell's wife had a baby. I bet that gobsmacked him."

She laughed, her eyes lighting. Anna had been one of the few young women not interested in the Campbells in school. Too full of themselves, she'd said.

"I came to beg you to come with me to my appointment at AGCT," Callie said. "If Ms. Scary Businesswoman Marvin can see I have a competent vet on board, she might give us that big grant we need."

"Sure, I'll come, but I think you're worrying too much." Anna clattered her metal rasps into her case and closed up her portable forge. "You have Ross Campbell eating out of your hand, and he's the brother of A, G, C, and T."

Callie's face flushed hotter than it had a right to. "First of all, he's not eating out of my hand. Second, it wouldn't matter if he were. Karen's not stupid—she's going to assess whether our idea is viable or we're dreaming."

"Okay, but I think the Campbells will love to say they're handing out money to the Joneses."

"And I don't want this thing to go because I'm a Jones," Callie said in frustration.

"Why not?" Anna blinked at Callie in her frank way. Her timidity when she was younger had hidden a shrewd mind. Somewhere along the way—probably in vet school and then fighting to prove she could succeed—she'd lost much of her reticence. "Use every asset you have. The important thing is rescuing and taking care of the horses, right?"

"Damn it." Callie growled. "I hate it when you talk sense to me."

"No, you don't." Anna's grin flashed, then cut off as a pickup pulling a horse trailer came down the lane into the wide dirt lot. "Shit. What does *he* want?"

He turned out to be Kyle Malory. He parked and hopped out of the truck, his affable look fading when he saw Anna.

Kyle's older brother, Ray, stepped down from the passenger side, but Anna didn't appear to notice him.

"Checking up on me?" Anna asked Kyle, planting her hands on her hips. "I told you, I'm keeping an eye on her for a couple more days to make sure everything's fine."

Kyle flushed a dull red. "I didn't come to take her back. Just to look in on her."

Anne flung a gesture at the trailer. "Yeah? Then why the transportation?"

"We dropped off a couple of horses at the rodeo grounds. You were on the way back."

Now Anna went bright red. She opened and closed her mouth, then said a subdued, "Yeah, well. Maybe."

Ray came to stand next to Callie. He was a broad-bodied man, compact but strong. He and Kyle were bull riders, and they trained cutting horses in the off season. Everyone in town, including Callie's dad, sent their cutters to the Malorys.

Kyle and Ray had dark hair and green eyes, and the River-bend females who didn't swoon over the Campbells swooned over them. Of course, many women were happy to gaze upon both—they weren't picky.

"One of our horses is preggers," Ray said quietly to Callie. "She was having some trouble, and Anna wants to make sure both mare and foal stay healthy before she sends them back home. Kyle worries like an old man."

Callie watched Anna and Kyle face each other, both
flushed, hands on hips, each trying to figure out what to say.

"I think it was an excuse to come over," Callie whispered
to Ray.

Ray huffed a laugh. "I think you're right."

Callie and Ray exchanged a quick glance of amusement.
Callie wondered if she was that obvious when she was around
Ross. Probably.

"Kyle," Ray called. "Say good-bye. We haven't got all day."
He winked at Callie and settled his hat. "Nice to see you,
Callie. You staying in Riverbend now?"

"Hope so," Callie said. "I feel kind of lame living in my
parents' house. I might look for a place of my own."

"We live in *our* parents' house," Ray pointed out. "It's not
such a bad thing."

Kyle and Ray owned and ran the Malory ranch now that
their father had passed and their mother had remarried and
moved with her new husband to Austin.

"True," Callie agreed. It wasn't so bad being home.

Ray tipped his hat to her and walked away, calling again
to Kyle.

Kyle finally stalked to the truck and got in. He waited for
Ray to settle himself in the passenger seat, then Kyle backed
the trailer with a competence of long experience, and turned
onto the road. Ray raised a hand in farewell through the open
window.

"He drives me crazy!" Anna shouted.

She rarely yelled—she told people what to do in a firm,
quiet voice. Men twice her size said a quick, "Yes, ma'am,"
when Anna talked.

Anna waved fists in the air. "He knows damn well I can
take care of that mare. He just wants to be a pain in my ass."

Callie calmly watched Anna's face go through every shade
of red and then resolve into a blotchy paleness.

"Mmm-hmm," Callie said, keeping her grin to herself. "So,

can I pick you up for the appointment, or will you meet me there?"

CALLIE CREDITED ANNA'S PRESENCE FOR THE FACT THAT Karen brought out the paperwork to start the grant process at that afternoon's meeting.

Or maybe it was the baby pictures Callie had sent Karen, or the fact that she'd driven Tyler to be at his wife's bedside before she gave birth.

Probably all those factors together, Callie decided. She hugged Anna after the meeting, the two high-fiving in the reception area in front of a brand new arrangement of flowers.

Anna had her rounds to finish, so Callie called Nicole from her car to tell her the good news. It would take time and work, but they might have the rehab ranch up and running soon.

She also texted Ross — *We got it!* He didn't reply for a time, but then, he'd be at work by now.

Knew you would, he responded as she was pulling around the drive at home. *Want to grab dinner?*

Sure. Meet you at the diner?

It's a date.

Callie stared at the last line for a long time. Had he been off-the-cuff responding or did he really mean a date?

And why was she beating herself up like this? She liked Ross and they were meeting for dinner. That was all. She would go and enjoy it.

It was only four, and Ross had said he didn't leave work until seven that day, so Callie put on riding clothes and walked out of the house in breeches and knee boots.

Manny rose from where he'd been sitting behind a porch post.

Callie shrieked, then pressed her hand to her chest and took a deep breath. "Shit, Manny. Don't *do* that."

"Sorry," Manny said cheerfully. "Thought you saw me."

He'd been back to help out the stable hands with chores a few times since his lawn-mowing incident, but she hadn't expected him today.

"I'd fix you some tea, but I'm going riding," she said. "Need to keep in practice."

"That's okay. I came to talk to you."

"Sure thing. What do you need?"

Callie started for the stables, and Manny loped sideways next to her.

"It's about Ross. I'm worried."

Manny's voice held a note Callie didn't like. She halted abruptly. "Why?"

"He's running for sheriff, right?"

"He's thinking about it," Callie said. News traveled fast. "Not sure if he's officially announced it."

"Well, tell him to stop." Manny drew close, glancing around as though someone might hear them across the huge stretch of lawn. "Some guys say if he doesn't withdraw—if Ross don't quit his job altogether—they're gonna shoot him."

Chapter Thirteen

C allie's heart squeezed with sudden fear. "What are you talking about? Who will?"

"Guys." Manny balled his big fists, his brows drawn. "I can't tell you. They'll shoot me too."

"Yes, you certainly can tell me," Callie said sternly. "This is a big threat, Manny. Life and death." She tried to gentle her tone. "I appreciate you coming to me, but you have to tell Ross what you know."

"*You* talk to Ross. He'll listen to you. He might not believe me, and I can't be seen with him."

"I'll warn him, don't you worry," Callie said. "But you have to say what you know and who these guys are. If you want him to be careful, he has to understand the exact danger."

Manny looked close to tears. "I'm not supposed to know anything. I'm just the lookout. The nobody. They'll come after me."

He was working himself into a panic. Callie didn't dismiss the danger—as the daughter of a locally powerful man, she was familiar with death threats. Resentment was a strong thing, and people let it get out of control. Each threat had been taken seriously and reported to the sheriff's office, not that Hennessey had ever taken them too seriously.

Callie remembered the local paper's headline of the day before — *Sheriff Runs Drug Gang out of River County.* A photo had shown an empty house, and the writer claimed Sheriff Hennessy and his brave deputies had kept River County safe for its residents.

"Does this have anything to do with that raid on the house in White Fork?" she asked.

Manny's stricken look meant she'd guessed right. "Those guys aren't there anymore," he said quickly.

"I'm betting they're still around, though."

Another fearful glance.

"Tell you what, Manny. I'll talk and you nod or shake your head. That way, you're not telling me squat."

Manny folded his arms. "Okay. I guess I can do that."

"Are they mad at Ross for the raid?" Callie asked. She received a head shake in the negative. "No? But they're mad at him for thinking about running for sheriff?"

A nod.

"Why?" Callie asked, then held up her hand. "I forgot. Let me keep guessing. Because Hennessy lets people get away with shit and Ross won't?"

An emphatic nod. Callie's breath deserted her a moment.

The implications of Manny's answer were legion. It might be nothing, and Manny might have misunderstood, but if he was correct, it pointed to corruption.

The criminals had deserted the house before the sheriff's department had shown up, the newspaper had said. Could that mean they'd been tipped off? Ross hadn't said much about the raid when he'd talked to Callie in the clinic cafeteria, nothing more than she'd read in the paper, but Manny's worry spoke volumes.

What if someone in the sheriff's office had warned them? Ross hadn't known about the raid before Mildred had called him, which meant that the other deputies probably hadn't either. But of course, Hennessy had.

What if the criminals, knowing they'd avoid capture while Hennessy was in office, had realized that Ross winning an election would mean the end of their free ride? They must believe Ross had a good chance, or else they wouldn't bother with him.

"Thanks for coming to me, Manny," Callie said, her heart beating faster. "I'll tell him."

"Keep my name out of it," Manny said. "Ross might come looking or me, and that would put him in more danger. If they think he has a direct line to information, they won't wait."

"I'll take care of it." She touched Manny's arm, which seemed to calm him. "But you do *me* a favor. Stop working for those guys, and men like them. It isn't worth your life."

Manny swallowed. "You're probably right, but I can't mow your yard every day, and anyway, your gardener will get mad. No one will hire me, and I can't blame them. What those guys give me at least keeps the electricity on. My dad hasn't worked in years."

Callie's anger flared—at Manny's father for not taking care of his son, at the drug dealers who kept Manny tied to them with the money he needed. At Ross for not taking Manny away from his situation sooner, at the entire town for not noticing Manny needed help. She grew mad at herself for the same reason.

"You know what?" she said, hands balling. "I'm going to need a lot of assistance getting the rehab ranch up and running. I'll hire you to help take care of the horses and make sure their stalls are clean every day and the feed doesn't run out. Sort of a stable manager. Starting now. All right with you?"

Manny's eyes widened as she spoke. "Seriously? *Me*? Are you crazy?"

"You've already proved you're a hard worker and reliable. You show up and do a job without fussing. We can negotiate a salary—it will depend on what we get in the grant, but we asked for several paid positions. The only thing you have to do for me is finish school. You didn't graduate, did you?"

"Nope. Didn't have time for it."

"The deal is, you go back to school this fall and you come work for me in the afternoons. If you need help with your schoolwork, I can do that or find you a tutor. But you *will* graduate, you *will* get a job, and you *will* win the respect of River-bend. All right?"

Manny's eyes went wider still, and his grin returned. "I'm really smart, promise. I can pass the tests—I just never bothered to show up for them."

"It will be part of the job," Callie said, trying to sound stern, but Manny's good humor was infectious, and she wanted to hug him instead.

"You got it. You're awesome, Callie. Tell Ross to marry you, and everything will be all right."

Callie laughed, but nervously. "I'm seeing him tonight. But not for marriage. I don't think."

"If he doesn't marry you, he's seriously stupider than I thought."

Manny started to run off, but Callie stopped him. "No, you don't. You work for me now. I meant it that I don't want you going back to those men. Starting right this minute."

Manny's smile died. "If I don't show up today, they'll know."

"You said they think you're a nobody, a lookout they pay whenever you're around. If you simply stop being around, they'll forget about you."

He shrugged. "Maybe."

"Then stay here, go down to the barn, and tell them I said to find chores for you to do. I'm going to call Ross."

Manny stared at her for a few heartbeats. Then, as though finally believing that his life might change, he leapt into the air.

When he came down he ran with youthful energy for the stable.

Callie called Ross on his cell phone but it went to voice mail. She tried to keep her voice calm as she left a message for him to call her as soon as possible. He was at work, she told herself. Probably not taking personal calls.

She understood why Ross wanted to keep things casual with her. He had a dangerous job. If they made their relationship serious, then every time Ross didn't answer his phone she was going to worry like crazy.

Too late, she realized sadly as she clicked off the phone. She was worried sick, which meant things had already gone far beyond casual.

"ROSS, YOU'VE GOT A VISITOR." MILDRED, HER HEADPHONES and mike hanging around her neck, moved past Ross's desk to the coffee machine. Ross's pulse jumped.

Callie? What was she doing here?

It could only be Callie, from Mildred's knowing look. If the visitor were his mother or brothers, Mildred would say.

His chair banged into the wall as he rose, which made Sanchez look up from his computer with an inquiring glance. Ross silenced him with a glare and moved through the thick door that separated the bowels of the sheriff's department from the rest of the courthouse.

It was a quiet day in the waiting room, no DUIs arguing that they were fine to drive, really, or Mrs. Kellerson complaining that her twenty-something neighbor—male—was sunbathing in the nude again. Mrs. Kellerson didn't mind so much, but her husband accused her of staring every time the man was out, and it was wrecking her marriage.

Callie stood on the other side of the counter, her face composed, her brown and blond hair caught in a sleek bun.

"Hey." Ross tried to sound neutral and friendly.

"Hey, yourself. Is there somewhere we can talk? It's important."

Callie wore riding clothes—that is, English style's idea of riding clothes—breeches and jodhpur boots, a smooth T-shirt, slim gloves tucked into her belt. She was only missing a helmet.

Her eyes bore agitation, and Ross decided not to tease her. He took her by the elbow and steered her behind the counter and into a small interview room. "You okay?"

Callie stood straight, the breeches and shirt outlining every inch of her body. Something to be said for English riding togs. Suede patches lined the insides of her legs, tempting Ross to run his hands over them.

"I am, but you're not," Callie said. "Manny came to see me, all upset."

With Manny that could mean anything from his father needing a hospital to him being wrongly accused of shoplifting.

"About what?"

Callie rubbed one fist with her other hand. "He's right to be. Someone's threatening you."

With succinct words, Callie told him that the gang who'd ditched town would target Ross if he ran for sheriff. Her eyes held fear, deep and unfeigned.

Ross rested his hands on her shoulders, liking the strong but soft body under her sleek shirt. "I hate to break this to you, sugar, but I get threatened all the time. A hazard of being a deputy. I take it seriously—don't worry—but I don't let it stop me."

"Yes, but ..." Callie glanced around, as though afraid of being overheard.

Which could happen. These rooms were miked and contained cameras, and though Ross hadn't flipped any switches, they could be controlled in the small room behind them.

"My shift's almost done," Ross said. "We were going to meet for dinner anyway. See you at Mrs. Ward's?"

Callie shook her head. "How about the library?"

Ross blinked. "You know, in my whole life, a girl has never asked me to go on a date to the library."

Her eyes softened, as Ross had intended. He didn't like how stiff her fear made her.

"It's quiet, is all I meant. Library closes at eight, but by seven, it's a ghost town. We can talk. Dena will make sure we're not disturbed."

"First-name basis with the town librarian. I'm moving in some snooty circles now."

"When you're shy and books are your refuge, you get to know the librarian. Dena's been friends with me for years."

Ross took a step back and looked her up and down. Callie touched her face, as she did whenever he regarded her closely.

"What?" she asked in trepidation.

"I'm trying to wrap my brain around Callie Jones being shy. Miss Debutante Homecoming Queen."

"I was only homecoming queen because people wanted to suck up to my dad. That doesn't upset me—I'm realistic. Parents told their kids to vote for me, nothing more."

"No, it's because you look good in a tiara, waving like the Queen." Ross demonstrated a royal wave.

Callie dissolved into laughter. "You are such a shit."

"And you're too hard on yourself. You were beautiful and generous—even neurotic, self-centered teenage kids understood that. You had my vote, with a big red X in your box."

Ross flashed her a grin, and Callie flushed. "You're still the charming Campbell, aren't you? Smiling like there's nothing wrong in the world."

"Not while I'm standing next to you."

Her blush deepened. "Laying it on with a trowel. I'll see you at the library."

"I'll be there. Callie," Ross added as Callie started to leave.

"Thank you for telling me. For taking the time to come all the way down here, I mean."

Her answering look stole most of his breath. "I owe you big time, Ross. I'd do anything for you."

The rest of his breath left him with her declaration, which was delivered with a shrug and a careless smile.

Somehow, Ross got the door open for her and ushered her out, managing to walk on his feet down the short hall. The passage was narrow, and Callie's hip bumped him time and again. The ever-efficient Deputy Campbell was about to become a puddle of useless sludge.

Hennessy stepped out of his office in time to see Ross open the door to lead Callie to the front. His dark eyes narrowed.

"Socialize on your own time, Campbell," he snarled.

Ross chose not to answer, but Callie turned her best gracious look on the sheriff. "I came to make a report, Sheriff. Lost horse. My daddy will be unhappy if it doesn't turn up. All done now. Please say hello to your wife for me."

Ross held his laughter in check until he got Callie out through the counter door and into the main lobby of the courthouse.

"Now, who's the shit?" he asked in her ear. Telling the sheriff to say hi to his wife had been the perfect finishing touch.

"I was just being polite." Callie leaned to him conspiratorially. "Don't let anyone go looking for a lost horse, though. I couldn't think of anything else to say."

"Don't you worry, sweetheart. I'll tell them you called back and said he turned up."

"She."

Ross frowned. "Sorry?"

"*She* turned up. It's the mares that go walkabout when any get loose. The geldings like to stick close to home. Mares have minds of their own."

"Do they?"

Callie's answering smile made the danger of him falling down return. "Oh, they do. See you later."

Watching her walk, the breeches outlining her curves, was like all Ross's dreams coming true. She gave a little wave over her shoulder to him, completing his meltdown.

Other men in the lobby glanced after her in appreciation. Ross scowled at them until they suddenly remembered they had other things to do.

This was going to be his whole life, he realized. Beating other guys away from Callie.

He had an advantage, though—he could always arrest them.

He'd have to lock up half the county, in that case. But if that kept her safe, he'd do it in a heartbeat.

RIVERBEND'S LIBRARY WAS A SQUARE BUILDING constructed at the beginning of the last century to house books for the entire county. Two floors held the collection, with a beautiful spindled staircase leading from one level to the next.

The librarian, a solidly built woman who dyed her gray hair red with blue streaks, sat behind a polished wooden desk near the entrance. Like a sergeant who knew the whereabouts of every single one of her troops, she directed patrons to find what they needed with exactitude. Callie was certain Dena could point to where each book in the library lay and had probably read them all.

Callie waited for Ross upstairs in the fiction section, having told Dena to send him up when he arrived. Dena, who was Mrs. Ward's best friend and had given Callie, aged six, her first library card, said she'd be delighted to.

The second floor held the fiction stacks. Callie knew exactly where each genre was shelved, alphabetically by author, as they had been for the last twenty-odd years. Right now she was in the *C*'s in mystery, pulling out her favorite Agatha Christies and thumbing through them. She liked the stories that featured the hyper-efficient secretary, Miss Lemon, especially the one in which Hercule Poirot learns Miss Lemon is human enough to not only make mistakes in her typing, but also to have a sister.

Callie was a few chapters into *Hickory Dickory Death* when she heard a firm step. She snapped the book closed and slid it back into its precise spot, forgetting all about the story at the sight of Ross closing in on her.

He'd changed out of his uniform, but he must have done it in a hurry because the collar of his button-down shirt was folded under in one corner and his hair was mussed.

Callie didn't stop herself reaching to smooth the collar. "Thanks for coming."

"Thanks for waiting." Ross's eyes were warm blue in the library's gloom.

I'll always wait for you, Callie wanted to say but didn't.

"Agatha Christie." Ross glanced at the shelves beside them. "I hear she was an expert on poison."

"She was," Callie said. "I grew up on her books." She leaned to him and whispered, "What I wanted to say in private was I think Hennessy tipped off the dealers in White Fork that you were going to raid them."

Ross's mouth set in a grim line. "Yeah, I wouldn't be surprised."

Callie's eyes widened. "Does everyone but me know he's corrupt?"

"Suspect," Ross corrected her. "We suspect, but it's hard to prove. He's very careful."

"Well, *you* be careful. This is dangerous."

"Sweetheart, I've been dealing with dangerous people all my life. You've met my brothers."

He was trying to make her laugh, to diffuse the situation as he always did.

Callie rested her hand on his chest, liking that it felt natural to touch him. "I worry about you."

Ross didn't move. "That's real sweet. And thank you for the tip." He went silent a moment. "But the real reason I rushed over is so I can ask about something else you said."

His eyes darkened, and Callie's heartbeat sped. "What's that?"

"That you'd do anything for me." Ross's gaze fixed her in place, his lashes very black. "What does this *anything* consist of?"

His voice was like velvet in the musty air. Ross didn't move, didn't touch her, only held her with a look and a question.

Callie swallowed. Something in the very back of her brain asked in panic, *You're not going there, are you?*

The tired, lonely, fed-up, young woman even deeper inside snapped back, *Yeah, I'm going there.*

She grabbed Ross by the lapels of his shirt, dragged him into the nearest study carrel, slammed the door, and then unbuckled and unbuttoned his pants.

Chapter Fourteen

✦

Callie pushed Ross against the table in the tiny chamber, which library patrons could reserve for quiet study. Callie remembered coming here her senior year, right before finals, to cram.

School wouldn't be starting for weeks, it was almost closing time, and the top floor of the library was deserted.

Her heart hammering, Callie jerked down the zipper of Ross's jeans, sliding her hand to the warmth inside.

Ross shook with laughter, which abruptly ceased as Callie closed her fingers around his smooth cock.

"Shit," he whispered.

Callie didn't give him time to say more. She stepped close to him, rose on tiptoe, and kissed his mouth.

She stumbled as he met her kiss with a hard one of his own, but Ross caught her in his arms. His little moan as she stroked him made her knees weaken.

Ross's strong grip held her up, his mouth on hers let her know her attack was welcome. Callie had made love with this man, but she'd not had enough time to explore him, to discover every fascinating aspect of his body.

He was as big as his belt buckle promised. Callie ran her hand the length of him, her blood heating when he sucked in his breath. His balls tightened under her hand, wiry hair tickling her fingers.

"Callie." The word was a groan. *"Shit."*

"You said that before," she whispered.

"Look at you. Doing a deputy in a … whatever this is."

"Study carrel."

"Study carrel. Fuck of a time to learn new vocabulary."

Callie leaned into him, pressing him back. Ross slid himself up onto the table without dislodging Callie's hand and leaned back on his elbows. He was a delectable sight, his jeans and underwear sagging down tight thighs, his eyes half closed, a sinful smile on his lips.

"Didn't you ever use a study carrel?" she asked in a soft voice.

"Nope. Never studied."

Ross, Callie had heard, unlike his four older brothers, had actually made good grades. A quick mind, Callie reasoned. He took in a situation, absorbed it, and understood it while others fumbled around.

He'd obviously caught on to her intentions fast and had no inclination to stop her. If Callie wanted to be bad in the middle of the library, his dark smile said, so be it.

Callie popped open the buttons of his shirt so she could kiss his skin. His chest rose under her lips as she kissed her way down, frantically pulling aside cloth.

She pressed a kiss to his navel, then below it, her lips lingering. He tasted of salt and heat, his body hard but smooth.

"Damn, girl." Ross's fingers moved in her hair, pulling it free of the scünci that bound it.

"Woman," Callie breathed, brushing kisses to his lower abdomen. "Not girl."

"You betcha. Oh, *fuck.*"

He groaned the last as Callie licked his tip. Then she opened her mouth and drew him inside.

Ross clenched one fist beside her. He ran strong fingers through her hair but didn't drag her down, letting her lick and taste.

She couldn't believe she was with Ross Campbell, in the library, alone in the dim light of a dying Texas day, doing *this*. He filled her mouth with hard goodness, the taste of him spicy. She liked how he felt under her tongue, hot and smooth, hard and slick. She took more of him, stretching her mouth to fit him.

Callie had never done this before, but she knew the theory. Her fiancé had been too fastidious to have wicked, dirty sex. Ross, the county deputy, the "good" Campbell, didn't seem to mind at all.

He made a noise of pleasure as she started to suck, his body moving under her touch.

No sound reached Callie from without, the library well and truly silent. She heard only Ross's breathing and her own, his whispered groans. She imagined a fictional librarian jerking open the door, finger to her lips, distressed only that they made any noise at all. She started to laugh, a fun thing to do with Ross in her mouth.

Ross said her name again, his voice gravelly. Callie eased back and looked up at him as he moved one hand behind his head, his face soft with pleasure.

This incredibly gorgeous man was spread out for her, welcoming her touch, wanting it.

"You said we should see where this thing we have goes," she said, giving him a slow smile. "I'm following my impulses."

"I like your impulses." Ross watched her with languid eyes. "You are the most beautiful woman I've ever seen."

Callie's heart squeezed, and for a moment, she couldn't speak. She tried to remind herself that she was coming off being deeply hurt, and she couldn't trust her own emotions, but her engagement seemed long ago, the memories fuzzy. Ross was erasing all thoughts of what's-his-name.

She quickly bent to him before she said anything stupid, and once more filled her mouth with him. Wonderful, wonderful man, hard and wanting her.

"Son of a bitch." Ross's words jerked from him. His hand landed in her hair, but he didn't push, didn't demand. "Sweet Callie. You're going to make me come."

Callie flushed in excitement. She wanted to taste him, feel him pour into her. She'd never thought about such things before, and now she craved them with Ross.

A soft chime made Callie jump hard. She yanked herself away from him, backing in the tiny space until she met the cool wooden door.

"The library will be closing in five minutes," Dena's quiet voice came over the loudspeaker. "Please make sure you check out materials before you leave."

Callie sucked in a shaking breath. She was in a public library, and Dena would come up here looking for them if they didn't soon go downstairs.

Ross groaned, then he laughed. He slid himself off the table and grabbed his jeans, sounds of mirth doubling as he smacked into the shelves intended for students' books.

He pulled up his jeans, zipping and buttoning them. "Her timing sucks," he said. "Cold shower for me."

"Or I could come to your place," Callie said. Might as well keep on following those impulses. "It's not far."

"Well, I'm not going anywhere else for a while, that's for sure." He chuckled as he pulled Callie into his arms and kissed her, at first tenderly, then more thoroughly.

They pulled apart as the chime sounded again. Dena usually didn't use a second chime, but she must know they'd be untangling themselves up here. Callie went hot with embarrassment, but at the same time, she wasn't ashamed. Ross made wicked sex seem natural and right.

She watched Ross button his shirt and tuck it in, then do up his belt, closing the large buckle in place. "Do me a favor, Callie. Walk between me and anyone we see. Please?"

His laughter continued as they went down the stairs. Dena said a smooth good night, but her look told Callie she'd deduced Callie was falling in love with Ross, and she approved.

They stepped out into Hill Country twilight, Ross wrapping Callie in as much warmth as the July sunshine.

SEVERAL HOURS LATER, ROSS LAY BY CALLIE'S SIDE AFTER an intense round of sex, their bare bodies entwined. Ross traced lazy patterns on her skin, following with slow kisses as he let the fact that he was with this amazing woman sink into his brain.

She wasn't the Callie Jones he'd lusted after in school, the out-of-reach angel, the one Ross shouldn't mess up with his touch. If he'd known what a warmhearted person she truly was, he wouldn't have chickened out asking her to the home-coming dance that day. He'd covered by saying he wanted her class notes. So feeble.

This Callie was sweet, smart, funny, had lots of courage, and was seriously sexy. Okay, so the sexy part hadn't changed.

When she smiled at him, warm with afterglow, Ross knew that Callie walking away from him would be the hardest thing he ever faced.

Ross slid over her again, bunching her blond-brown hair in his fingers as she welcomed him inside. His thoughts dissolved to simple joy, and they loved each other hard and fast.

When daylight seeped through the windows, Ross opened his eyes to Callie waking up next to him. Best morning ever.

They showered together and ate Ross's home-cooked breakfast of eggs and sausage, toast and roasted potatoes.

Callie dressed again in her riding clothes—it would be all over town Callie hadn't gone home since she'd come running to visit him at the sheriff's department, but oh well. His neighbors could suck it.

They kissed goodbye in Ross's garage where Callie had left her car. Because the door was closed, Ross indulged in a long, deep kiss while he ran his hands over the fabric stretched across Callie's lovely ass.

She partook in the kiss with equal enthusiasm, cupping his backside in return.

They were laughing as they parted, Ross giving her one last kiss before she made it into her car. The silver Mercedes slid down the square in the bright sunshine and turned the corner to head east out of town.

Ross let out a breath, smoothed his uniform, and walked across the square to the county courthouse.

He ignored the knowing looks—an indulgent one from Mildred—and Sanchez's and Harrison's teasing, and walked down the hall of the sheriff's department, knocking politely on the door marked *Noah Hennessy, Sheriff, River County*.

Hennessy was at his desk, reading correspondence on his computer. Or maybe playing video games—Ross couldn't tell from this angle.

"What is it, Campbell?" Hennessy asked impatiently. Maybe he was about to reach his next level.

"I thought it only fair to warn you," Ross began.

His tone caught Hennessy's attention. His head snapped up, his game—or work—forgotten. "Warn me about what?"

Ross straightened his spine. "I've decided to throw my hat into the ring and run for county sheriff. I wanted to tell you before I go in and make it official."

Hennessy's eyes narrowed. Ross, for the first time since he'd worked at the department, had the man's full attention.

"Running for office is no joke, Campbell," Hennessy said in his slow, condescending drawl. "Campaigning costs money.

Signs and flyers alone are hellacious expensive, and I warn you, any donor is going to expect you to do what they want, damn what you think is right."

Was that what had happened to Sheriff Hennessy? He was at the mercy of his campaign donors? Had drug money elected River County's sheriff?

Absolutely nothing had come from the raid in White Fork. Even the cell phone Harrison had found had been pre-paid with the charges used up and call history erased. Still waiting for fingerprint and DNA results on it, but Ross expected nothing usable. He reasoned the thugs wouldn't have left the phone if it could point to them in any way. They'd been well and truly warned.

"I appreciate the advice," Ross said. "But I've decided."

Hennessy rose, his bulk making his chair creak. "All right then. Thank you for your courtesy. Do me a favor and clean out your desk before you go. Leave your badge and gun with McGregor."

Ross remained still. "So, you're firing me?" As predicted, but he'd half-hoped the sheriff would take the high road.

"I'm giving you the opportunity to resign. Conflict of interest. I can't have insubordination in the office or the possibility that you'll disobey an order and endanger me or your fellow deputies."

"I've never done that," Ross said, keeping hold of his temper. "Nothing has changed."

"Oh, running for office changes a man, Campbell. You'll learn that. It's your choice. Drop the idea and go back to your job, or run against me and get out."

Rage, doubt, disgust, and rage again ran through Ross. The most even-tempered Campbell balled his fists as the choice dangled before him.

Ross loved his job, always had. He helped people, whether they knew it or not, whether they thanked him or not. It gave him a sense of purpose, even on the most boring stakeouts or long days filled with paperwork. The idea of not walking across the square to his desk every day, shooting the breeze with Sanchez, arguing with McGregor, slowly making friends with Harrison, opened an empty pit before him.

He'd chosen long ago not to be a stunt-riding cowboy, to take a job he considered meaningful.

What would he be if he hung up his badge? If Ross lost the election, Hennessy would never let him come back. He'd fill Ross's place and move on, leaving Ross to crawl home to his family and try to figure out what to do next.

On the other hand, the Sheriff of River County was taking kickbacks from drug dealers and placating his campaign supporters instead of keeping the citizens of Riverbend, White Fork, and surrounding communities safe.

If Ross wanted to help people, the first thing to do was get rid of the corrupt sheriff.

He looked Hennessy in the eye, and made his choice.

"All right then," he said with slow steadiness. "Please accept my resignation. It's been great working for you."

He didn't wait for Hennessy's reaction, only turned and walked out of the office, squaring his shoulders as he went.

CALLIE SAILED OVER THE CROSSBAR ON HER FAVORITE horse, Sunny, who landed squarely and cantered on the correct lead to the next low fence.

She loved this—the wind in her face, the mare moving beneath her, Callie balancing for every jump. Riding was her life. She couldn't believe she'd almost given it up to live in manicured suburbia.

Sunny landed perfectly on the other side of the next fence, and Callie patted her. "Good girl."

She turned the mare for cooling laps, and saw Ross standing by the gate.

Callie stiffened, and Sunny, picking up her agitation, danced sideways. Callie calmed her with another pat, surprised at herself for losing her composure.

But he looked so damn hot. Ross had shucked his uniform for jeans and a T-shirt, boots, and a cowboy hat, its brim shielding his face from the bright Texas sunshine.

She'd left him only a few hours ago. Unable to settle down in the house, Callie had put on fresh riding clothes and headed to the stables. Manny was there already, helping to clean out stalls, groom horses, and carry bales of hay to the mangers.

He poked his head out of the barn in curiosity, but Callie was glad to see Manny continued working instead of dropping everything to watch.

Callie slowed Sunny to a walk and continued around the ring before coming to a halt.

"Mr. Campbell," she said, loosening her helmet as she looked down at him. "What brings you here?"

"You call that a saddle?" Ross asked, pushing back his hat to study the Wintec beneath her. "I call it a pot holder."

"I'm not strapping a huge Western saddle onto my best jumper and taking her around a course," Callie said calmly. "Might as well use a park bench. But wait 'til you see me in my Western getup, cowboy. I won my barrel racing ribbons fair and square."

"I know you did." Ross's warm look made her heat. Callie had been proud of her gymkhana days. "You looked hot in your pigtails."

Callie slid out of the stirrups, swung her right leg behind her, leaned on the saddle, and moved smoothly to the ground, landing on both feet.

"I'd pay to see you ride in an English saddle, hotshot," she said.

Ross's brows lifted. Before she could answer, he hung his hat on a post and swiftly climbed the fence, his movements economical.

His cowboy boot looked wrong in the iron stirrup, but Ross swung himself up onto the mare without disturbing her. Sunny looked around at him, wondering at the stranger on her back, but she settled immediately, knowing a competent rider when she felt one.

Callie adjusted the left stirrup for him, very aware of the strength of Ross's leg hanging next to her, the tightness of his thigh at her eye level. Pretending nonchalance, she went around to adjust his right stirrup.

Ross fitted the reins under his thumbs and out beneath his pinkies without Callie having to tell him. No trying to neck rein with the snaffle bit.

She eyed him in suspicion. "You've done this before."

"When I was twelve, I made the mistake of telling a champion jumper I thought English riding was sissy. He schooled me. Literally. I took a year of lessons with him."

"I never knew that," Callie said in surprise.

"I kept it a deep, dark secret. But it taught me respect. And how to stay on a horse without relying on my park bench saddle to keep me there." Ross turned Sunny to put her into a walk then a smart trot, rising and falling in a competent post.

"By the way," Ross said as he rode past, his very nice butt going up and down in even rhythm. "I filed the paperwork to run for sheriff today. And Hennessy fired me."

"What?"

Callie started forward, but Ross nudged Sunny into a canter. He executed a perfect turn, rode at the low crossbars, and eased Sunny over it in a neat jump.

"Ross!"

Ross cantered to the corner, turned the mare, and rode to the second jump. Sunny changed leads on cue and prettily rose over the fence, ears pricked, Ross low on her back.

Horse and rider moved as one, and Callie spent a moment drinking him in.

As he slowed the horse and walked her over to Callie, she wiped a bit of drool from the corner of her mouth.

"Fired you?" she choked out when Ross dismounted with the ease of long practice.

"Yep." Ross drew the mare's reins over her head and folded them competently in his hand. "I either win, or I have no job in the sheriff's department." He shrugged. "Course I won't have a paycheck now, so I'll have to move back in with my mom. How lame is that? Grown man, living with his parents."

Callie had said much the same thing to Ray Malory, but the twinkle in Ross's eyes told Callie he didn't really mind. Carter and his family had their own wing in the Campbell's ranch house, and Tyler had until recently been living in the apartment over the garage. The Campbell family home was like the Jones's—anyone welcome, anytime.

"You don't have to worry about money," Callie said before she could stop herself. "I have some. Enough to support us, anyway." Her mouth kept moving, Callie in alarm hearing her own words come out. "Marry me and I'll help you run your campaign."

Chapter Fifteen

All feeling left Ross's body. He was seventeen again, covering up his awkwardness by swaggering and shrugging while he lost the courage to ask the girl of his dreams on a date.

The girl of his dreams had just said, "Marry me," like it meant nothing.

Except it meant everything.

Callie flushed bright red. "Ross. Damn. I didn't mean that. I don't know why I said that. I'm not trying to trap you—"

Ross grabbed Callie by the shoulders and stilled her words with a kiss.

Callie stiffened, but she kissed him back, her mouth shaking. She tasted of dust and warmth, perspiration and agitation, but she sought him with mouth and lips, and pulled him close.

The mare's nose bumped Ross. He eased from the kiss to find the horse eyeing them curiously, wondering why the humans had crushed their faces together.

He let out a chuckle and nuzzled the mare's cheek. "*She* thinks it's a good idea."

"Ross, really, I don't know why I—"

Ross touched his fingers to Callie's lips. "It's not a terrible thought. I'm liking it."

Callie shook her head. "We're not ready for that—*I'm* not ready. I told you, I didn't want to use you on the rebound, hurt you ..."

"Callie—"

"Let me finish. You wanted to take things slow, see what happened. Asking you to marry me is so not taking it slow ..."

"Doesn't matter." Ross touched her mouth again, liking the satin of her lips, the heat of her breath. "You're right. We team up. It was your idea for me to run against Hennessy, a good one."

"We can team up without getting married." Callie sounded desperate now. "I'll fund your campaign. I want to."

Ross shook his head. "No, save it for your rehab ranch. You need to put all your money into that."

"I know how to budget, plus the grant from your family's charity will go entirely to the ranch, with Nicole in charge of that funding. It will be a totally separate thing. You just tell me how much you need, and I'll donate that."

"That easy, is it?" Anger slowly replaced Ross's elation. "What is this, a business proposition? Well, damn, darlin', I thought you asked me to marry you because you liked me."

"I do like you. I mean ..." Callie trailed off and wet her lips. "More than like. I'm trying not to coerce you into something you don't want to do. My dad can't stand Hennessy and would be happy to help you oust him."

"While his daughter decides whether or not to keep going to bed with me?" Ross scowled. "Forget it."

"Ross, I didn't mean ..."

Ross wasn't stupid enough to explode in rage while a horse stood next to him. He contained himself long enough to lead the mare through the gate, signaling to Callie's stablemen to come fetch her.

The one who loped to them was Manny. Manny's jeans

were dusty but whole, his T-shirt with a *Jumping J Ranch* logo on it was likewise unripped. He stood a little straighter, and his eyes were clear, as though he'd gotten some decent sleep.

"Yeah, I work here now." Manny gave Ross a proud if smartass look as he took the mare's reins. "Callie gave me a job. A real one."

Callie nodded as though Ross needed confirmation. She folded her arms, obviously uncomfortable.

Manny gazed back and forth between them. "Looks like you lovebirds need to talk. I'll get back to it then."

He led the mare away, breaking into a soft whistle as he walked her to the barn.

"That was real nice of you," Ross said, gentling his tone.

Callie shrugged. "I know he might run off when he gets bored, but he needs someone to take a chance on him, to show they trust him."

"Yeah, he does. But you aren't getting out of this argument because you're so damn nice. That's how it started — you trying to be nice."

"Offering to fund your campaign? Oh, I'm so sorry. Real thoughtless of me."

"No, offering to *marry* me to fund my campaign. And then taking it back in the next heartbeat."

"Because I thought you wouldn't want that!" Callie shouted. "*You* were the one who said *This is nothing. Keep it casual. Not important.*"

"The hell I ever said you weren't important." Ross remembered spouting the other stuff though, like a dickhead.

"It's what you meant." Callie's eyes flashed fury. "You gave me that sexy smile and said our sleeping together was just having fun, didn't mean anything. Ross Campbell having it all his own way."

"Where are you getting this?" Ross glared at her even as he rapidly went over the scene in his head. He'd learned long ago how to get his big, tough brothers to do anything for him, and he hoped like hell he hadn't tried the same techniques on Callie. "I had to say something with you standing there apologizing for sleeping with me, like I was a notch on your bedpost or something."

"A notch on *my* bedpost?" Callie's blue eyes widened. "I'm surprised *your* bedposts can still hold up your mattress. Everyone knows Ross is a love-em and leave-em kind of guy. I didn't want *you* to think I was another of your conquests, or that I was happy with your pity fuck."

"You think that's what it was?" Ross heard himself roar. Ross never yelled. Said exactly what he thought, pointedly, but he never shouted. He didn't have to. "A *pity* fuck?"

Callie balled her hands. "It's what you let me know it was. Poor Callie got left at the altar. I'll let her do the rebound thing with me so she doesn't feel like such a loser."

"Are you shitting me? What the hell kind of person do you think I am?"

"A Campbell. Everyone knows they do exactly what they want, and don't care that a woman is eating her heart out over them."

Was Callie saying *she* ate her heart out? No, not her. Not the cool debutante with the hospitable smile who'd held her head high and faced the town after she'd been publicly jilted.

"What was I supposed to say to one of the cool-as-snow Jones girls?" Ross demanded. "One of the we're-richer-and-better-than-anyone-in-the-county family? *Oh, thank you for blessing me with your presence?* For deigning to get your hands dirty with a cowboy? Who was giving the pity fuck?"

"Son of a bitch, Ross—here I was thinking you were the kind of guy I could have an actual conversation with, who didn't care about my family. I thought you saw me as *me*. I guess I was deluding myself with a hell of a lot of wishful thinking."

"I *do* see you as your own person, damn it. I hate that asshole who took away your confidence. I see you as a beautiful, smart, generous woman I want to know better. And I'm not gonna marry you so you can bestow the gift of your money and family on me. I don't want that from you. I want *you*. And I told you before I didn't believe in friends with benefits. I want a lot more than that with you. A hell of a lot more."

Callie had drawn a breath to keep arguing, but now she stared at him, red lips parted. "I didn't know that."

Her simple statement made Ross tamp down his hot words. Of course she hadn't known what he felt about her. He'd lain there and told her they'd keep things cool, not rush into a relationship.

He realized now that he'd already been falling in love with her, and trying to keep it from her so he wouldn't look like a total fool.

Ross drew a breath. "I guess the question is, what do *you* want?"

Callie's chest rose, stretching her tight riding shirt in enticing ways. Ross's need flared, but he clenched his hands and didn't reach for her. He had the feeling he'd ruin everything if he did.

"I don't know," she said, the words soft. "I think I haven't known my whole life."

Her words touched his heart, stirring feelings long suppressed. Growing up in the shadow of talented, well-liked, sought-after brothers hadn't been easy for Ross. Everyone had expected him to become a clone of them, follow in their footsteps, be another Adam or Grant or Tyler, to be like them in both the good ways and the bad.

Carter alone had seen Ross as his own person, and that only because Ross had been young and vulnerable, bringing out the protectiveness in the damaged Carter. Ross had saved Carter from himself, and Carter had taught Ross the courage to pick his own direction.

Callie had gone through the same thing, Ross realized with a jolt. She was a Jones, rich and privileged, and because of that, the world placed her in a box and put the lid on it. She wasn't allowed to be anything other than a Jones girl, her future mapped out for her. Why she'd want something other than being a man's pampered plaything was beyond anyone's comprehension.

Never mind Callie's own hopes and dreams, her needs as a human being. She wasn't allowed to have those. By these rules, Callie's place was as fixed as Manny's—if she chose to give it up and work at what she wanted, she was ungrateful. If Manny chose to work at what he wanted, he wasn't trusted.

"Callie," Ross began.

Callie squared her shoulders. She didn't fold into herself, but the look in her eyes shut him out.

"Could you please leave, Ross?" she asked. "I need to think about a lot of things."

"Shit." Ross's curse was a whisper, and he knew he'd just blown it with her, irreparably.

Somehow they'd gone from friends to maybe in love to uneasy acquaintances in the space of ten minutes.

"Sure." Ross retrieved his hat from the post, brushed it off, and plopped it on his head. "You want to talk to me, you call me."

He made himself turn from her sad face and hurt-filled eyes and walk away.

He'd only gone ten paces when his feet turned him around again. "I mean that. You can talk to me about anything, anytime. Even how much you hate me. Don't care if it's the middle of the night. I don't have a job now. I'll be home."

She only looked at him, still as a marble statue. Her riding togs outlined a body Ross had dreamed of holding on to for a long time to come.

Once more, he made himself turn and go. He caught sight of Manny as he walked toward the truck he'd arrived in—Carter's—he'd had to borrow it. Manny opened his mouth, his entire body betraying his distress that Ross hadn't swept Callie off her feet and carried her away.

Ross shook his head at Manny, but he knew the kid was right. He should have done just that.

It was a hell of a thing to take a perfectly good life and fuck it up as much as Ross had done today.

"YOU OKAY?"

Callie jerked her head up to see Anna standing by one of the pillars on the shady back veranda. Callie had retreated there once Ross had gone in a cloud of dust. She'd had the idea to fix herself an iced tea and think about things, but once she'd reached the porch, she'd collapsed into a chair, too numb to move.

"I don't know," she said truthfully as Anna leaned against the pillar and watched her. Anna's boots were covered with dust, as were her jeans, though she'd obviously washed up a little down at the stables.

With all the animals on the Jones ranch, Anna was a frequent visitor, and at the moment, Callie was grateful for her presence.

"Did Ross piss you off?" Anna asked. "He seems like such an easygoing guy."

Callie came to her feet in frustration. "He is easygoing. I pissed *him* off. Which backfired on me. I am seriously confused …"

"No, you're not," Anna said. "You're in love with him."

Callie stared at her. "I can't be. I'm brokenhearted. I was dumped. I'm working through my pain." The words came out in a monotone, and Anna laughed.

"You forget, I was at that wedding. I remember your fiancé declaring he was too busy to wait for you, and me thinking you were better off if he went. Pretty much everyone thought so too."

"I've come to that conclusion," Callie admitted. "But still, being humiliated in front of a couple hundred people is not easy to take."

"Honey, I saw your face when your sisters told you Devon was gone. You were shocked, naturally, because who stands up a bride on her wedding day? You were angry too—I'd have been spitting nails. But you also looked relieved. Like you'd talked yourself into marrying the guy and now you were off the hook."

Callie blinked at her, startled. "I did?"

"Yep. And instead of collapsing into a sobbing puddle, too heartbroken to go on, you ran down the steps and jumped in the truck of the gorgeous Ross Campbell. You know what Karen Marvin said? 'Hey, that was smart.'"

Callie bit back a laugh as Anna's words penetrated her numbness. She tried to remember exactly what she'd felt when Montana had said, "Sweetie, he's gone. I'm so sorry."

She'd been stunned, embarrassed with all those people around her, and furious. She'd agreed to marry Devon and put up with a lot of his shit, believing she had to make allowances for him because he was a successful businessman and didn't have lots of time for people.

She'd been angry that her sisters had let her down, mad at the rain, and outraged that Devon hadn't had the patience to wait a mere hour or so for his own wedding. Callie had sought the one person she'd known could comfort her. Ross.

Callie sucked in a breath as she realized Anna was right. In the moment her sister had told her, in the seconds before mortification had overcome her, Callie had been relieved.

Relieved she wouldn't have to listen to Devon belittling the rehab ranch, or Riverbend, or her family and friends, or anything else important to her. She'd seen her friends' husbands—including Trina's—tear them down so often, she'd started to believe it was normal. What husbands did. Her father had never done such a thing to her mother, but they were an older generation. Maybe times had changed.

Devon would have ridden her until he'd broken her spirit.

Ross never would.

"Oh, shit, Anna, what the hell did I just do?" Callie dropped into her chair, face in her hands. "I practically told Ross to get the hell out of my life, when he's the best thing that's been in it for years!"

She heard the scrape of a porch chair and then Anna's work-worn hands covered Callie's and eased them down.

"Talk to him, sweetie. Ross actually seems like a reasonable guy. You've had a lot happen to you—I bet he'll understand if you're real nice about it."

"Eat humble pie, you mean."

"If that's what it takes. Not too humble, though. You don't need to stroke his ego."

Callie blew out her breath and leaned back in the chair. "He told me to call him when I figured myself out. I'm picturing myself choking when he answers the phone. I won't know what to say. At all."

"It will come to you. Just be sweet. Tell him he's cute and adorable and you can't stop thinking about him."

Callie laughed weakly. "He won't believe me."

"He's a guy, honey. Yes, he will."

Callie continued to laugh, feeling a little better. "You are so cynical."

"I've been around the block. The Campbells, from what I've seen, are susceptible to flattery."

Callie sent Anna an interested look. "I can see you're not into stunt riders. Bull riders, now—that's more your style."

She was rewarded by watching the unflappable Anna go beet red and look anywhere but at Callie.

"I don't know what you're talking about," Anna mumbled.

"Don't worry. Your secret is safe with me."

Anna swiftly unbent to her feet. "What's to like about bull riders? It's a stupidly dangerous sport, they can break every bone in their bodies, and it's hard on the bulls."

"Tell you what," Callie said, getting up with her. "Become a rodeo clown. That way you can help the rider and make sure no harm comes to the bull."

Instead of laughing like she was supposed to, Anna looked thoughtful. "You know ..."

"I was joking," Callie said quickly. "Joking. Dangerous."

Anna nodded, a little too readily. "You're right. Letting that go. You sure you're okay, Callie? I have to get on with my calls."

Callie knew an excuse to depart when she heard it. If Anna'd had that many stops to make, she'd have left right away. She didn't like to make sick animals wait.

"I'll be fine." Callie let out a breath. "You've both cheered me up and given me good advice. Now I just need to figure out how to act on it."

"Like I said, Ross seems to be a reasonable guy. See ya, Callie."

Anna gave her the briefest of hugs then she hurried down the veranda and back to the stables where she'd parked her truck.

Callie watched her drive out, a little too fast. She knew she was right about Anna's absorption with Kyle Malory—this would be interesting to watch.

She groaned and sank back to the chair. Callie needed to sort out her own love life before she tried to fix everyone else's.

———

ROSS SPENT THE REST OF THE DAY PUTTING THINGS IN order for his coming campaign. He hung on to Carter's truck, reflecting that he'd need to buy his own truck or motorcycle to get him around. He hadn't bothered, living so close to work and groceries.

He hadn't been a civilian since the few months between graduating from high school and swearing in as a sheriff's deputy. He'd fit commuting to college for his criminal justice degree around the job. Being unemployed would take some getting used to.

Keeping busy and planning the rest of his life helped him not think about Callie — almost. His gut churned every time he pictured her beautiful face, the confusion in her eyes when he'd yelled at her that he didn't want her half-assed marriage proposal.

Not how it was supposed to happen. Ross had planned to win the election by a landslide then run to her, go down on one knee, and hand her the biggest diamond ring he could find.

The bottom had fallen out of his world when she'd said, *Marry me and I'll help you run your campaign.* As though the marriage part of that suggestion wasn't important.

It kept falling, like an endless pit. Ross pounded the steering wheel and scrubbed a hand through his hair.

"What am I — *stupid*? The most beautiful girl in the world asked me to marry her, and I said *No*? Son of fucking bitch!"

Callie wasn't a desperate, sad woman needing a man, any man to make her feel better. She was over that asshole — Ross could see it in her eyes. Callie had a family behind her, her own life, her own money. She didn't need Ross, and that worried him.

Why? Because he was afraid he had nothing to offer? Nothing that would keep her by his side? What the hell was wrong with him?

Callie liked him, had said she wanted to be with him. That should have been enough for Ross.

But no, he wanted her to fall in love with him, as hard and strong as he'd fallen in love with her.

In the end, Callie had told him to go away.

Maybe she'd call. He'd told her to call. His phone lay beside him, ready to be answered.

"I am so fucking pathetic," Ross said out loud. "Fucking dumbass." His brothers had been right. He hadn't taken Callie seriously enough.

Ross drove around until he couldn't think of any excuse to not go home. He'd have to move out soon—he could manage a couple more months rent before he ran out of money.

His mom planned to use the apartment over the garage at Circle C as a guest house now that Tyler and Jess and family had their own home. The small, two-room place with refurbished kitchen and bath was good for a bachelor.

"Because I'm going to be a bachelor for the rest of my sorry life," Ross muttered as he pulled into the alley. He'd have to return Carter's truck tomorrow. Ross now had no vehicle and no job, and soon, he'd have no home of his own.

"Dumb fuck," he told himself.

He opened the garage door and slid Carter's truck into the small space.

The passenger door was yanked open, and a man Ross knew only from reputation slid inside.

Ross never locked his doors when he drove around, because, well, this was Riverbend. Everyone knew everyone else, and besides, a would-be carjacker might find himself looking at the business end of a loaded shotgun.

The back doors of Carter's big cab also opened to admit two very large men.

"Ross Campbell?" his front-seat passenger asked. He wore a gray suit with a bolero tie and one tasteful ring on his right hand. His hair was dark brown, his eyes a piercing blue, and he set his cowboy hat on the seat between them. "I'm Dell. Let's go for a ride, shall we?"

Chapter Sixteen

Ross gazed back at Dell Leith, the biggest drug dealer in the Hill Country. Because Ross had turned in his badge that morning, he no longer had to say "alleged" drug dealer. Dell was the man, and everyone knew it.

Ross also couldn't pull out a gun and wave it at Dell, because he'd turned in his pistol with the badge, and Carter didn't carry firearms in his vehicle.

Another man who'd been in the shadows of the garage pried open the truck's hood and looked around inside before he lowered it again. Searching for a tracker, Ross suspected. He wouldn't find one there.

Dell had already taken Ross's cell phone, and he handed it out the window to his thug, who tucked it into a pocket. It was likely he'd carry the phone a long way in the opposite direction to where Dell took Ross before he smashed it.

Ross leaned out the window. "Hey, if my girlfriend calls, tell her I said sorry and that I'll call her back as soon as I can." He turned to Dell and pasted on a smile. "We kinda had a fight."

"I'm sorry to hear that." Dell flicked his fingers at his lackey who faded away. "Let's go, Mr. Campbell."

Ross knew damn well the thugs in the back had guns trained on him. He sighed, put the truck in reverse, and started backing out of the garage. "Where to?"

"I'll let you choose the route," Dell said easily. "You'll feel more comfortable that way. Don't worry. If all goes well, you'll be back here in time to call your girlfriend and make up."

"Uh-huh," Ross said skeptically. "Okay, then."

Dell rolled up the window as Ross drove sedately down the alley and around the square. The closed passenger window would keep people from seeing Dell clearly, and the men in the back were shadows.

Ross hung his arm out his open window, ignoring the heat. He pulled to a stop on the far side of the square, facing the road that would take them northward out of town.

Ray Malory crossed the street in front of them. He glanced at Ross, noting that he drove Carter's truck and that a man sat next to him.

He gave Ross a little nod of recognition, which Ross returned, and Ray continued walking.

Ray, the oldest Malory, spoke in a lazy drawl, enjoyed beer, and moved in slow deliberation, but he wasn't stupid. He'd seen Dell and registered him, but didn't betray, by look or pace, any alarm. He continued to the feed store on the corner, raising his hand in greeting to the owner.

"Who's that?" Dell asked as Ross pulled away.

"Him? Oh, Ray. Hates the Campbells. We've been rivals for years."

"You don't say."

Ross didn't respond. Dell gazed out the window, as though interested in the last buildings in Riverbend and then the ranch country that unfolded around them.

It was beautiful in the late evening, the worst of the heat fading, clouds glazed golden by the afternoon sun.

Ross turned down a fork off the main road, heading for the river. The Colorado took a wide bend through the county just there, hence the name of the town. The bluffs at the end of the road made for a great picnic and hiking area, with dirt roads that led down to swimming holes and places to fish. The greenbelt along the river was officially a state park, which kept it pristine and let wildlife flourish.

It was one of Ross's favorite places to go when he needed to think. He'd planned to bring Callie there on one of their "dates," to stroll by the river, lie in the shade of spreading trees, kiss and enjoy the calm, maybe make love if no one was around.

Not that he'd had any days off to do this—although now, Ross had endless time. That is, if Dell's guys didn't shoot him and push the truck off a bluff.

Ross hated that such violent people marred the beauty of his county, but here they were. Courtesy of Hennessy.

"So, what you want to talk about?" Ross fell into easy tones, as though he wasn't worried. He was just a stupid country boy in his boots and cowboy hat. He couldn't be all that smart, could he?

"You," Dell said smoothly. "And your application to run for sheriff. Go back to your courthouse, withdraw your name, and we'll leave you alone."

"I see. Not a fan, are you?"

"Mmph." The sound held humor. "You're out of your depth, Campbell. You're very young to run for a position of such responsibility."

"Minimum requirement is twenty-one in this county. I looked it up. Clean record, experience in law enforcement helpful. My brothers were the ones who drove pickups into storefronts and TP'd the mayor's house. I was the good one, always stayed home and studied."

Another grunt. Dell didn't dress like a gangster or act like everyone's idea of one — he could be another good old boy busi-nessman at the bar.

That's how he perceived himself, Ross understood. Just a businessman. His commodity was heroin or cocaine instead of software or cloud storage or feed and tack. He dealt in cash rather than credit and drifted into and out of the county, setting up in decent neighborhoods. Dell didn't sell out of his house directly but had a network of kids who delivered the stuff and took the money.

Manny had been one of his recruits. For that, Dell would pay.

They reached the hills around the river, and the road began to wind. A drive with stunning views, one of Ross's favorites.

"Say what you need to," Ross said, fingers sliding along the steering wheel. "I'm listening."

Dell shrugged. "Not much to say. I prefer Hennessy to remain sheriff."

Ross's hairline grew damp with perspiration. The open window let in a draft of hot air, good excuse for the sweat trickling down his temples.

"Hennessy's getting on in life," Ross said. "He'll retire soon. There'll be a new sheriff in a few years, whether you like it or not."

"Probably." Dell didn't seem worried. "My bet is on McGregor."

"Could be." Ross imagined Hennessy grooming his favorite to take over. "But what's wrong with me? I'm young, like you say, so I have a shot of staying in for a long time, if the people of River County like me."

Dell's voice turned grim. "What's wrong is *I* don't like you. You rag on Hennessy too much. Guy's just trying to do his job."

"Hennessy is supposed to work for the county. Turns out, he's working for you too, right?"

"Did he tell you that?"

"'Course not. I deduced it. The only way you skedaddled out of that house in White Fork is if he told you he was coming. And the only way he'd have told you is if he was getting paid. Hennessy is kind of greedy."

"Let me be blunt with you, Mr. Campbell, instead of talking around the point," Dell said in a hard voice. "Hennessy understands his situation. *You* have a lot of family in River County—all those brothers who are now breeding children. Plus many friends. Plus that pretty young woman you're chasing around from the big ranch."

Ross went cold, his uneasiness and perspiration vanishing in a heartbeat. Dell Leith had just made a very big mistake.

"Son, her daddy can eat you for breakfast," Ross told him, letting his drawl deepen.

Dell gave him a minute nod. "I think both you and he will do as I say, for her sake."

Big, *big* mistake.

Not much traffic out here this late, the road now rising from the meadows to wind around stands of trees, the Hill Country at its most magnificent.

"Why all the threats?" Ross asked, keeping his voice easy. "You did a deal with Hennessy. Why not offer me the same terms?"

Dell's eyes were cold, like ball bearings behind human lenses. "Nice try. I know what entrapment is."

Ross lifted one hand from the wheel. "What entrapment? I no longer work for the sheriff's department. I turned in my badge and gun, remember? My uniform is at the cleaners. And like hell I'm going to tell Hennessy anything that's said in this truck. It belongs to my brother, anyway."

Dell studied him a moment. He'd taken Ross's phone, this wasn't a police vehicle, and there was little chance anyone was listening in. "Let's say a hundred grand a quarter. Cash. For nothing. Leave me the hell alone and have someone tell me if anyone gets the great idea to flush me out. I don't do anything illegal in the nice suburban homes I rent."

Ross believed him, but he pretended to think. "A hundred a quarter is thirty-three grand a month. In my present circumstances, I'm going to need a little more."

"Seriously?" Dell smiled, but no warmth reached his eyes. "You're a shithead, but all right. Fifty a month until you are elected. Then your salary will have to cover your expenses."

"Wait a minute. Once I get elected, I get a pay cut? That's no incentive."

"You have balls, Campbell. Okay, fifty a month, in perpetuity, and I ensure you push out Hennessy at the ballot box."

"You have that kind of money?" Ross asked him. "And that kind of pull? I was messing with you."

"You have no idea. Hennessy was happy with thirty grand, but I guess you like your comforts." Dell glanced out the front window. "I don't like to tell you your job, Deputy, but you're taking these curves a little fast."

Ross took both hands off the wheel, accelerated into a hairpin turn, and then slammed his hands back down to swing the truck around the corner at the last minute. The back tires skidded, heading for the road's edge.

"Don't worry. I've been driving back here since I got my license." Since before that, in truth, when Carter had taught thirteen-year-old Ross on these roads, but Ross wasn't going to say that out loud.

Another very tight curve approached. Ross dragged the truck around the corner and sped up still more.

"Seriously, Campbell, what are you doing?" Dell said, some alarm in his voice. "My guys will shoot you dead."

"Yeah? While I'm doing *this*?"

He let the truck roar off the highway, the pickup nearly airborne until it landed, spinning and dancing, on a smaller dirt road. Ross righted the wheels and drove on at a high speed, keeping his turns tight as the road wound down the side of a steep hill. A ravine opened up on the right, the river sparkling at the bottom.

"Shit!" Dell finally lost his reserve. "You asshole—are you crazy?"

Ross's voice went grim. "If your guys shoot me, you're not going to be doing too well. I'm not sure the passenger side airbag works. Carter gets busy, forgets to fix things." Ross lied —the airbag was fine, because no way in hell would Carter let his wife or daughter ride with him if it wasn't.

One of the men in the back was green, sweat shining on his face. Ross had been watching his motion sickness come on. The other man just looked scared.

"You might want to tell them to take their fingers off the triggers," Ross said. "To avoid accidents."

He swerved the truck to the edge, sending rocks and dirt spewing into the ravine, before he pulled it back at the last second.

Dell motioned to his guys, and Ross heard the clicks of safeties being engaged. "I swear to God, you are a dead man, Campbell."

"Why? I thought we had a deal. This is just me having some fun."

Ross spun around another corner, back tires tearing into soft earth.

Ross had driven this road hundreds of times, in vehicles both larger and less sturdy than this, including his sheriff's SUV. Kids liked to come down this way to raise hell, each generation believing they'd found the secret spot to party at the bottom of the canyon. Adam told Ross their dad had come down here in his teens to enjoy a few beers. Probably their grandfather had come in his day, to smoke rolled cigarettes and drink bootleg whisky.

He knew Dell would have his men shoot him the moment he stopped, so Ross decided not to stop. Not until he was good and ready.

Another blind corner reared up, and Ross gunned the engine. Rocks littered the road, a perfect ramp. He punched the accelerator as hard as he could, and the pickup left the ground.

"SHIT. SHIT—CALLIE, IT'S ME!"

Callie had set down her fork on the breakfast bar, not really wanting the plate of pasta she'd fixed for herself. She'd cooked because she knew she needed to eat, but she had no interest in food. She'd listlessly picked up the phone when it rang from an unknown number, but now she came alert.

"Manny? Calm down, sweetie. What's wrong?"

She wondered if his dad was ill, or if the man had thrown Manny out. No matter—the Joneses kept trailers for the hands who lived on the ranch, and one was empty. Callie had meant to offer it to Manny, but much had happened today, and he'd gone on home after the horses had been fed.

"It's Ross," Manny said in a frightened voice. "They're gonna kill him."

"What?" Callie's focus sharpened. "Who is?"

"Dell—the guy the sheriff pretended to chase out of White Fork. He's got Ross. I saw him in Ross's garage. I was hiding there, and Dell and his thugs walked in. I about shit my pants."

Callie dimly wondered why Manny had hidden himself in Ross's garage, but she'd ask him about that later. "Tell me what happened. Exactly."

"Ross pulled in, Dell and his guys got into the truck, and they all drove away. Except for the guy who took Ross's phone. He walked out and went to the diner."

"Is he still there?"

"At the diner? Yeah. But Dell has Ross. They drove out of town. They're going to kill him!"

Callie believed him. If Hennessy was taking kickbacks

from this man called Dell, and Ross had decided to run for sheriff, Dell would see that as a threat. He probably figured Ross knew about Hennessy's corruption.

Fear chilled her. Ross was alone, and these men were serious business. They wouldn't think twice about killing him —they'd waited until he was no longer under the protection of the sheriff's department to grab him.

If Ross died, Callie knew her life wouldn't be worth living. Devon leaving her had been a blow, an infuriating one, but she'd not grieved for him. Lying low in her parents' house had let her lick her wounds and figure out what she wanted to do, but she hadn't shed many tears, not for Devon. Even ending her friendship with Trina hadn't upset her the way it should have—Trina hadn't tried to get back in touch since the day of the barbecue, her abandonment of Callie final. Trina's friendship, Callie realized, had been of the fair-weather kind.

Ross had infiltrated himself into her life, had become a strong thread in the weft of it. He'd always been there, she realized. Even their ridiculous fight this morning was only a blip in their road. They'd recover, figure out what they wanted, maybe have terrific make-up sex, and go on.

Callie would never recover if Ross was killed. Neither would his family. Neither would Manny—it would teeter him to the dark side, just when Ross was pulling him out of it.

"Manny, honey," Callie began, hoping her voice was calm. "Keep an eye on the man in the diner. Do *not* approach him, and if he leaves, let him go. I'm coming into town right now. Okay?"

"Don't worry—I don't got a death wish. But hurry. Ross is in shit so deep, I don't know if we can dig him out."

Manny's voice held tears. Callie dashed away her own as she hung up, grabbed her keys, and sprinted out the door. Her silver car roared to life, and she barreled down the drive to the highway.

With one hand, she thumbed Karen Marvin's name on her

phone, the only person close to the Campbells, besides Ross, whose number was in her contacts. It went immediately to voice mail, but Callie shouted at her to get hold of the Campbell family and tell them what had happened.

She dropped the phone on the seat and stomped on the gas. The little car shot faster than it ever had across the miles into Riverbend.

MANNY WAS TERRIFIED.

Inside the diner, the man who'd occasionally hired Manny to run errands and carry packages for Dell Leith calmly ate pie. Mrs. Ward and her staff had no idea—though they must be suspicious of the stranger. But Mrs. Ward wouldn't turn away a customer unless she knew good and well he was a bad guy.

Callie had said not to approach. Smart. The man might recognize Manny right off. He might not shoot Manny in public, but he could drag him off to the middle of nowhere and kill him. Dell's men had done such things before.

But Manny wasn't so much terrified for himself as he was for Ross.

He'd gone to Ross's apartment to yell at him to get his butt over to Callie's and make things up with her. She needed him. Ross needed her. What was there to figure out?

The garage had been unlocked, but the apartment above wasn't, so Manny decided to wait in the shade of the garage for Ross to come home. Then Dell had appeared out of nowhere.

Manny had spent the scariest twenty minutes of his life hiding in the corner behind the tool bench, praying Dell and his goons didn't spot him.

He'd forgotten about his own fears, though, when Dell had climbed into the truck with Ross and told him to drive. And Ross, damn it, had obeyed. Hadn't fought or anything.

Manny had known calling the sheriff or his deputies would do no good. Probably Hennessy himself, pissed off that Ross had decided to run for sheriff, had told Dell to off him.

Manny didn't have a phone number for the Campbells, but he could call Callie. She'd made sure, since he worked for her now, that he could get hold of her anytime.

The dude in the diner was shoveling in big forkfuls of pecan-studded whipped cream when Callie pulled her silver Mercedes into the parking lot. She hopped out and looked around for Manny but didn't see him. Of course not. He'd taken cover in the bushes.

Damn, she wasn't going inside to confront the thug, was she?

He relaxed as Callie walked out of the parking lot and across the street, then tensed again as she headed straight to the county courthouse. The main building was closed for the day, but the entrance to the sheriff's department was still unlocked. Callie strode to it and opened the door.

Manny stifled a curse, sprang from hiding, and ran as fast as he could across the square, catching the door before it swung shut behind Callie.

So, here he was, marching into the lion's den, ready to protect the first person who'd ever believed in him.

Chapter Seventeen

✦❦✦

M anny caught up to Callie before she could approach the counter at the sheriff's department, and grabbed her arm.

"What are you doing?" he whispered fiercely. "Hennessy's in on it."

"I know." Callie's eyes were hard, dangerous. Wow. Sweet, soft Callie had just turned into a dragon. "Hello," she said to the deputy on duty—Joe Harrison. The new guy.

Harrison gave her a look of polite inquiry, but also interest. Everyone knew Callie and Ross were doing it.

"Can I help you, ma'am?" Harrison asked.

"Yes. I'd like to report the kidnapping of Ross Campbell."

For a second, Harrison started to grin—he thought she was joking. Then his smile died. "Wait. You're serious."

"I am," Callie said. "*He* is a witness."

She pointed at Manny, who did his best to look like a granite pillar in the middle of the floor.

"Tell me what happened," Harrison said quickly, all business.

Callie pulled Manny forward with a surprisingly strong

hand, and Manny, for the second time that evening, launched into his tale.

"What?" Mildred the dispatcher had come forward as soon as Manny began speaking. "Are you sure?"

"Yeah." Tears of frustration sprang to Manny's eyes. Why was everyone being so slow? They needed to get after Ross.

"*I* believe him," Callie said. "Can we look for Ross, please?"

"Hell, yes." Harrison hit a button and told whoever was on the other side of the intercom to get in there. "Which way did they go when they left town?" he asked Manny. "Did you see?"

"North." Manny balled his fists. "Hurry. They're gonna kill him!"

Deputy Sanchez raced in. "What the fuck?"

"I'll call all the dispatchers in the Hill Country," Mildred said, bustling back to her desk. "We'll put out a BOLO."

Finally, someone was doing something. "They took his phone," Manny said. "Can't track him that way."

"I'll get my truck," Sanchez said. "Harrison, call the Campbells. Tell them what's happening. They need to know."

He didn't take two steps before Sheriff Hennessy appeared in the doorway. "Sanchez, stay where you are. Mildred, Harrison, don't call anyone. I'm not starting a panic on the word of this juvenile delinquent."

"Will you start it on *my* word, Sheriff?"

Callie was amazing. She stood straight and looked old Hennessy in the eye, radiating courage.

"No," Sheriff Hennessy said. "I won't, young lady."

Callie's brows shot up. "I see." She was poised in her jeans and T-shirt, a stain on the front showing she'd been eating tomato sauce of some kind. She refused to wilt under Hennessy's condescending stare. "Mr. Hennessy, a citizen of River County is in danger. I demand that you send someone to help him."

Manny wanted to punch the air. But Callie needed to be

careful. Hennessy might try to lock her up on some stupid excuse, like disturbing the peace, wasting police time …

Hennessy maintained his cool, as though daring Callie to make something of it. "He's probably gone off to sulk about being fired. When he's ready, he'll come back and let you kiss him better."

Uh oh. He shouldn't have said *that*. Callie up 'til now had been holding it together, but no, Sheriff Hennessy had to go and piss her off.

Callie's tones chilled about fifty degrees. "All right, then, Sheriff. I don't like to play the Jones card often, because it's embarrassing and somewhat rude. But my father is very influential in this town. If I tell him that Ross has been taken by a drug lord, and the sheriff can't be paid to care, that's not going to go down very well with him or his friends. The Campbells either. I wouldn't want to get on the bad side of *them*. My dad is, however, very good friends with the sheriff of the next county. If River County's next-door neighbor has to solve its problems, you're not going to come out of this well."

Hennessy's face darkened. "Don't you threaten me, missy …"

Callie took a few steps back and lifted her cell phone. "How about I give my dad a call? He's on a much-needed vacation, so he won't be happy to be disturbed."

"This is a fucking waste of time," Hennessy said. "Sanchez, get out there where this kid is pointing and take a sweep. You won't find anything, but what the hell? Mildred, don't you dare call anyone. Harrison, get back to what you were doing. Don't any of you tell the Campbells anything until we know more. All I need is the pack of them howling around here."

Manny craned his head to look around the room behind the counter. "Where's McGregor?"

"It's his night off," Hennessy snapped. "Lucky him. Now get out of my station."

Callie gave the sheriff one last glare and then marched out, her head high.

Manny ran after her, easily catching up. "I love you, Callie! You handled that like a boss."

Callie turned to him, her blue eyes full of tears. "Won't make a difference if we can't find Ross."

Manny laid his hand on her shoulder. "Hey, don't look like that. We'll find him. At least *I* will. I heard Dell telling Ross to pick the route. I think maybe I can guess where he went. He told me it's his special place. He's caught *me* there so many times, it's pathetic."

———

THE TRUCK LANDED, SKIDDED HARD, AND TORE AROUND another corner. A shouted curse came from a guy in the back — the other one had his eyes closed. Dell hung on to the dashboard, his face set.

Ross laughed. He knew this road like the back of his hand. It leaned out into the gulch here, pulled back into the trees there. He could drive it without his headlights if he had to.

"I'm gonna kill you." Dell snarled. The man had lost all his suaveness. Ross wouldn't be surprised if he were sitting in pee.

"That's what they all say." Ross slammed the truck around another hairpin turn.

The road ended on a pebbly beach next to the river, a gorgeous place on a hot summer day. Especially pretty when the sun set, staining the bluffs above in a red-golden light.

Ross knew that as soon as he stopped, one of the men in the backseat would jam his gun into Ross's neck and shoot him, happy to do it.

As Ross hit the open space by the river he popped his seatbelt buckle. The next moment, flung open his door. At the same time, he dove out, tucking and rolling as he hit the hard-packed earth.

The truck spun out of control and slammed into a stand of saplings. It broke a few and then lodged among them, the engine sputtering and dying as the front end dipped dangerously toward the flow of river.

Ross gritted his teeth, ignoring pain as he rolled. He finally came to a halt, unfolded to his feet, and ran, staggering, under the trees.

He looked back to see one of the thugs pry open the rear door and more or less fall out. The other crawled out after him. Dell was still in the front seat, alive or dead, Ross couldn't tell. He turned away and kept running.

Branches slapped at him, and he slipped in mud, but Ross went on. If he could elude Dell and his men long enough …

A pistol shot ripped through the air. They couldn't possibly see him in the dusk beneath the trees, but a man blindly firing might eventually hit something. Ross heard the *wang-wang* of bullets striking branches, coming too close.

Carter would not be happy about his truck. But Ross would kiss the man if he popped up now to yell at his baby brother.

Ross knew that on the far side of this stretch of woods, a rock outcropping jutted into the river. If he could reach it, he'd be sheltered from pinging bullets.

He didn't have a phone or radio, or any way to communicate except for shouting, and yelling would only pinpoint his location to Dell's goons. Ross prayed that his choice of destination, Ray Malory's perception, and the little switch he'd flicked under the steering wheel would lead his family to him. God bless his sister-in-law Bailey and her computer tech savvy.

A bullet struck the ground alongside his foot. *Shit.* Ross doubled his pace, his cowboy boots not made for running. His job, thankfully, had kept him fit, as did his workouts—not having a steady girlfriend ensured that he spent many evenings at the gym.

Still, the terrain was rough, Ross's feet were cramping, and he slipped and slid in dust as bullets rained around him.

The inlet of river was icy when he plunged into it up to his knees. Ross jumped as a shot struck the rock outcropping above his head.

He'd be visible for a moment in the river, in the dying sunlight, but if he made it, he'd be safe.

Ross slammed himself around the far side of the outcropping as chips of it exploded beside his head. His face stung with the cut of stone as he ducked back into shadows.

At the same time, he heard a drone of engines—not the rumble of trucks or SUVs, but the louder, earth-shaking thunder of motorcycles.

Ross grinned. The cavalry was coming.

He lost his smile as he realized he had no idea whether that cavalry was for him or Dell. He was a sitting duck, but he had to keep on sitting, if he wanted to live.

CALLIE PULLED BACK TO THE HIGHWAY AFTER SHE'D MOVED over so Sanchez's SUV could race past with lights flashing. She sped after him.

Not long later, headlights came up behind her, many of them, and fast. Callie's already sickening heartbeat heightened as motorcycle after motorcycle spilled over the hill and surrounded her car.

"Holy shit!" Manny peered out the window, eyes wide with fear. "They're gonna kill us."

"Don't be so dramatic," Callie said, but she worried he might be right.

That is, until she recognized one rider who hung on the back of a Harley, his face set in grim fury.

Relief swamped her. "That's Carter Sullivan," she said.

Then new worry hit her. Were they heading for a shootout? Would Ross survive it?

"Seriously cool." Manny bounced in the seat. "Go faster. Don't lose them!"

The motorcycles swarmed past, as though Callie's car was a boulder in a stream, and Callie stepped on the gas to keep up with them.

Her car was the street model of a racer, its engine engineered for speed. She easily moved with the motorcycles, not letting them out of her sight.

"You're a badass, Callie. If you rescue Ross, he'll have to marry you now."

"Why are you so adamant about us getting married?" Callie asked, trying to distract herself from her fears. "When I first saw you, Ross was arresting you."

"Because if he has *you* to run home to every night, he'll leave me the hell alone." Manny scrunched up his face. "That and the guy is so lonely. I kind of like him. He busts my balls, but he's always making sure I don't go to jail. He's trying to look out for me. No one else ever did."

Ross took care of everyone. He teased or growled, and he took no shit, but he'd made sure both Manny and Callie were all right that day in the pouring rain. He'd made sure Jess got to the clinic to have her baby, and that Callie wasn't left out of the celebration. He'd been there for her at every turn, for Manny as well. Ross might be the youngest Campbell and the quiet one, but she'd seen the respect his older brothers, especially Carter, accorded him.

Callie's heart warmed, at the same time her fear escalated. "Well, we'll just have to rescue him, won't we?"

The road wound in sinuous curves, heading for the river. Callie had been this way many times, with her sisters, with friends and boyfriends, back when life was carefree and full of endless possibilities.

When Sanchez's SUV and then the motorcycles plunged

off the road to the dirt track that led to the river bottom, Callie groaned. "You've got to be kidding me."

"Don't stop," Manny urged. "We need to help him."

Ross was down there, dead or injured, surrounded by men who had enough money to bribe a county sheriff to stay the hell out of their way.

Without stopping to think about it, Callie turned the car and bounced onto the washboard road. Manny whooped in elation.

How Sanchez and the motorcycle posse knew Ross was at the end of this track, Callie had no idea, but they didn't slow. One guy wiped out, but he got up and waved the others past. Callie pulled alongside him and stopped. "Get in."

Manny climbed into the back with the energy of youth so the man could slide into the passenger seat. He was Jack Hillman, a friend of Carter and of the Malory brothers. Jack, with his close-shaved beard, bandana, and tatts, was another of the "bad" boys Callie had been told to stay away from. Now Jack's dark eyes were filled with worry.

"Ray called me," he said. "Said Ross was being carjacked by Dell Leith. Asshole. We'd warned Dell to stay out of our town, but I guess he figured he was untouchable. If he's got Ross, Ross is screwed."

"Don't say that." Callie gripped the wheel as she started after the motorcycles again. "We're here to rescue him."

Jack grinned. "Awesome. But you should be turning around and driving out of here. Ain't no place for a lady."

"Tough shit," Callie said without slowing. "Ross is down there."

"So are a few armed gangsters, and a bunch of bikers with a grudge."

"And a deputy sheriff and Ross's brother. I'm not going home to do needlepoint while I wait for the men to come back and break the news to me."

Jack laughed. "You sure aren't like what I thought you'd

be, Callie."

"No one is. Smart of Ross to head for this place."

"You know about it?" Manny asked in amazement.

"I was a teenager once," Callie said. "Great place to come and make out, if you had a good enough truck to get up and down the road. My sisters and I rode our horses down here too."

"Horses would be better," Jack said, "but Carter didn't want to ride any into what might be a line of fire."

Callie caught up to the motorcycles, which were weaving and spinning with the road. Callie's car negotiated the curves well, but her throat was tight, her palms slick.

At the bottom, headlights lit the little beach by the river. A pickup truck was stuck, nose-down, in the trees above the swiftly flowing water, its back wheels at least three feet off the ground.

Sanchez was already out of his SUV, which he'd pulled in behind the pickup. He had his gun trained on a man in the truck's passenger seat, neither he nor the man inside moving. Stalemate.

Motorcycles swarmed the clearing. Guys stopped bikes and headed off for the woods, and Callie's heart jumped into her throat when she heard shots.

Her car slid sideways before it jerked to a halt. She stepped on the gas and the wheels spun, but the car went nowhere.

"Seriously?" She jammed on the brakes, the car fishtailing and miring deeper into the mud. Callie pounded on the steering wheel. "You do this *now*?"

Jack leapt out and ran after his friends. Manny climbed out in his wake.

Callie jumped from the car and landed in mud up to her ankles. "Manny, don't you dare."

"We have to help Ross!" Manny wailed.

Callie felt the same need to run around in the dark, calling out for Ross, but she knew that would do little good. She pried her feet free and seized Manny by the hand. "I'm not explaining to him how you got yourself killed running after him. You stay here and keep me safe."

Manny stared at her in anguish, but after a moment, understanding settled on his face. "Because if *you* get hurt, Ross will rip me a new one," he said, his voice softening. "What do we do, Callie?"

"Call for backup. Deputy Sanchez needs help." Callie pulled out her phone.

Backup was already there. Two more pickups came down the dirt road, moving carefully but swiftly.

The first truck disgorged Adam Campbell, the second, Grant and Tyler. Adam carried a shotgun. He strode to Sanchez's side, cocked the shotgun, and aimed it at the man in the cab.

The man inside at last raised his hands. Sanchez stepped to the cab, opened the door, and told the man to get out. He did so, his face dark with blood.

Sanchez cuffed him. "Dell Leith, I'm arresting you for kidnapping, carjacking, and extortion. Probably more things later."

"Good luck making the charges stick." The man's voice was smooth and unworried, though he looked banged up.

"They'll stick!" Manny yelled at him. "You're a total dirtbag, Leith. I know all kinds of things about you and your gang, and I'm not afraid to tell everyone I know!"

The cold in Dell's eyes was the same as what Callie had seen in Sheriff Hennessy's. Chilling.

More shots sounded in the woods, and then shouting. Cursing, yelling, and then the shots, and everything else, went silent.

Callie forgot about her warning to Manny, her promise to herself to be careful. She ran blindly forward, fear making her ill. If Ross was hurt, dying, she needed to be there. To hold him, comfort him, tell him how much she loved him.

She saw movement between the trees. This wasn't a thick woods, only a thin copse that surrounded the river, green and cool on a summer's day.

Motorcycle guys appeared, dragging between them two men who were bloody and bruised. No sign of weapons on them, and they looked a bit pathetic.

Behind them came Carter Sullivan, his hand firmly under the elbow of a limping Ross Campbell. Blood dripped from Ross's head, but his eyes blazed with triumph, and his grin was wide.

"Tell me you got all that, Carter," Ross was saying.

Callie had no idea what he meant, but Carter gave him a brief nod and said, "Yep."

Callie dashed past the hard-looking bikers, ignored the equally mean-looking Carter, and flung her arms around Ross.

Ross lifted her against him. "Hey, there, sugar," he said in surprise. "What are you doing down here? You should be safe and snug in your big old house."

"Shut up." Callie clung to him, shaking in gladness. "You're all right. I needed to know that you were all right."

"Aw," Ross said, his voice light. "You were worried about me?"

Callie let go of him. "Damn you, don't joke. Yes, I was worried—worried sick. Why wouldn't I be? I love you."

Ross's smile died, and his eyes went dark, anything teasing gone. His face was nicked and bruised, but otherwise, he looked whole and unhurt.

"Love …"

"You heard me." Callie dashed tears from her eyes. "I'm not afraid to say it. I don't know if it's what you want, but it doesn't matter. I still feel it."

"Of course I want it." Ross's eyes were clear, blue, intense. "Don't ever think I don't want it. I've wanted you to love me since I found you in the rain in a wedding dress ready to tie the knot with another man. You know how hard it was not to run off with you? To say to hell with him? Manny was right, I should have married you that day."

Callie's breath caught, a bubble of happiness pushing aside months of heartbreak and doubt. "I'd have done it. You were the only one I wanted to turn to. The only one I could."

Ross cupped her face, his thumbs on her lips. "I fell hard in love with you, Callie. And I haven't fallen out of it."

Callie couldn't speak. She kissed him, never minding the men swarming the woods, including Manny, Ross's brothers, Sanchez, and the thugs.

Ross frowned, worry clouding his eyes. "But shit, don't you ever do this again. These guys had guns and weren't afraid to use them."

Manny had halted a few feet away. "Cut her some slack, Ross. *She's* why Sanchez is here. She went right into the sheriff's department and bullied Hennessy to let Sanchez go after you."

"Don't you dare say you were fine," Callie said swiftly as Ross gaped at her. "You weren't fine. You needed help." Tears burned her eyes and clogged her throat.

"Callie …"

"Don't argue with her," Carter growled. "Just kiss her."

"Yeah," Manny agreed.

Ross's anger didn't evaporate, and she knew they'd fight about this later, but it didn't matter. He'd be alive to fight with, and Callie wasn't letting this man go ever again.

Ross gazed down at her a moment, then his smile returned, the charming one that had melted her all those years ago. He crushed her against him, and his mouth came down on hers, erasing fear, erasing pain.

Callie pulled him close and surrendered to the joy of kissing him.

Dimly she heard Carter, who'd moved to give them space. "Aw, shit," he said, fury in his voice. "Ross, what the *hell* did you do to my truck?"

Chapter Eighteen

I t was good to be home. Ross leaned back on the sofa in the big house at Circle C Ranch. He'd washed his face and tended his cuts and now relaxed while his brothers, sisters-in-law, nieces and nephews, and his mom, doted on him—and on Manny, who was basking in the attention.

Best of all was Callie, curled up on the couch next to Ross, her head on his shoulder. Ross stroked her sleek hair in tenderness, bending to press a kiss to it now and again.

"It's all good?" Carter rumbled to Bailey, Adam's wife.

Bailey, her dark hair pulled into a ponytail, tapped on a tablet, frowning over it. As Ross had suspected, she was pregnant with her and Adam's second child, and Adam hovered protectively nearby.

"Seems like it." Bailey raised her head with triumph as she tapped a button.

The rattle of Carter's truck and roar of the engine came to them, and then the words:

"You have balls, Campbell. Okay, fifty a month, in perpetuity, and I ensure you push out Hennessy at the ballot box."

"You have that kind of money? And that kind of pull? I was messing with you."

"You have no idea. Hennessy was happy with thirty grand, but I guess you like your comforts."

The entire family, and Callie, stared at Bailey in shock. But, Ross noted, not in surprise. They'd all suspected Hennessy was dirty.

Grant let out a whistle. "You got, on tape, a drug lord admitting he's paid off the sheriff of River County? Wow."

"I don't know if it will convict anyone," Ross said, shrugging. "Though I was a civilian when he told me this. I can turn the information over to a justice or another sheriff as a citizen doing his duty."

Adam gave Ross a slow nod. "No matter what, it will make Hennessy retire. The letter of the law is one thing. Public opinion is another."

Callie sank into Ross—fine with him. "How did you record that?" she asked. "I thought they took your phone and checked for trackers."

"Because they didn't realize what Carter had done to his truck." Ross laced his fingers through Callie's, liking how well they fit together. "Carter isn't a fan of earpieces or holding a cell phone while driving, so he asked Bailey to rig him up something that would let him talk to Grace or Faith while he's tooling around. Bailey used to be a techno-geek. She built a phone into the dashboard, which is activated by a little switch under the steering wheel. All I had to do was click it on, and it called Grace."

"Which scared the shit out of me," Grace said. She sat on a chair, her feet drawn up, while Carter lounged on the arm next to her. "I thought someone was threatening Carter—then I realized they were threatening Ross."

"Which was okay with you," Ross said, grinning at her.

Grace stuck her tongue out at him. "You know what I mean. I ran and got Carter from the stables, and he said Ray

Malory had already alerted him." Grace shuddered. "We were scared to death for you, Ross."

Callie snuggled into Ross, resting her hand on his chest. "I agree."

Ross kissed the top of her head. "I could be a smartass and say I wasn't worried, but I was. Scared I'd never come back and talk to Callie. Cause I really need to talk to her."

Adam took the hint—all the brothers did, because they rose abruptly. "Come on," Adam said. "Let's give baby brother some privacy."

"Not necessary." Ross stood up and held Callie's hands as he helped her to her feet.

Then he swallowed his pride, his nerves, and his uncertainty, and went down on one knee.

"Callie Jones," he said, looking up into her beautiful face. "Will you marry me?"

And please don't say No in front of my entire family. Or at least let me down easy, okay?

Callie's smile blossomed, warming his whole body. "I already asked *you* that."

"I know. And I stomped away like an idiot. I'm going to change my answer and say *yes*. What about you?"

Her chest rose with agitation. "Yes," she whispered. Then she laughed. "Yes!"

The room exploded in cheers. Campbell brothers hollered. Manny yelled "Awesome!" and fist-bumped Jess then Tyler. Manny whirled around the room, windmilling his arms, and Dominic tried to imitate him.

The next thing Ross knew, Callie was on her knees with him. Ross pulled her close, her softness and sweetness unwinding something tight inside him.

She kissed his mouth, and the resulting spark made Ross wish his brothers would suddenly remember something they had to do. But they didn't move. They were happy for him, wanting to stay and celebrate.

Ross stood up and pulled Callie to her feet, keeping her within the curve of his arm.

His apartment in town was too far away. He'd never be able to drive all the way home in his distracted state, and after what he'd done to Carter's truck, he was pretty sure his brothers wouldn't be lending him any vehicles anytime soon. Callie's car had been well stuck in the mud at the river, and was once again under the care of K.D. and his auto shop.

There was one place, however, and it was conveniently close.

"Excuse us," Ross said. "I'd like to speak to Callie in private."

Without waiting for a response from his family, Ross took Callie by the hand and led her out the front door.

"*Speak* to her," Grant said. "Is that what they're calling it these days?"

Ross ignored him. Callie's cheeks grew pink, but she laughed with Ross as they hastened down the porch steps and along the drive to the garage. A steep staircase led to the apartment above it, and Ross ascended without hesitation, towing Callie behind him.

The door was unlocked—no fumbling for keys—and Ross pulled Callie inside.

The two-roomed living space had been cleaned and aired, fresh sheets put on the bed. Olivia had told Ross he could occupy it whenever he was ready.

"What did you want to talk to me about?" Callie asked as Ross shut and locked the door. "I said yes already. Not taking it back. You don't have to persuade me." She gave him a severe look. "Not letting you take it back either."

"Grant is obnoxious, but he's right about one thing." Ross lifted her from her feet, cradling her against his chest. "I really didn't want to talk."

"Yeah? What did you want to do then?" Callie's beautifully

crooked nose wrinkled with her smile as she relaxed against him. "Cook me dinner?"

"Maybe later," Ross said as he ran with her into the bedroom. "Remember, I'm a terrific cook. But right now …"

He stilled her words with a kiss as he set her down. The kiss she answered him with, the one that said she truly loved him, made everything hard in him dissolve.

Except one part, which stayed pretty hard.

The bed waited. Ross didn't. There was a flurry of limbs and laughter as clothes came off, and then the flurry calmed. Ross and Callie eased down onto the sheets, their eyes on each other, then lips.

Ross heard the laughter of his family in the distance, but here was quietude, love, and Callie.

He kissed the woman of his dreams, surrounded himself in her as he slid inside, and at last found the happiness that had eluded him for far too long.

CALLIE WOKE TO MOONLIGHT. ROSS SLEPT NEXT TO HER IN the tumbled bed, sheets and pillows everywhere, his breathing even and deep.

For the first time in months, Callie knew peace.

She'd agreed to marry the hottest man in Riverbend, a man who truly looked at *her*, and with whom she could share laughter, love, and dreams.

She was on her way to funding her rehab ranch and helping her friend Nicole and also giving Manny the chance to have the life he deserved.

Ross would be sheriff and rid the county of the corrupt Hennessy. He'd win—she knew it. Callie saw many hostess duties in her future, but that didn't daunt her. She'd been trained to throw parties. She'd recruit her sisters and mom to help her, and Ross's family would be right behind her.

The road of her life straightened, no longer empty and bleak as it had been that rainy day in May when her car had plunged into a ditch and sealed her fate. Now the road was full of life, of hope, of love and Ross.

"Thank you," she whispered.

"Hmm?" came the sleepy question. "For what? The great sex? I should be thanking you."

Callie kissed his mouth. "For everything. I'm happy, is all."

"Me too." Ross ran his fingertip along her lips. "I can't tell you how amazing you are. I love you, Callie."

"I love you too." She sent him a smile. "I don't mind if you try to tell me how amazing. You're pretty amazing yourself."

Ross laughed. He rolled her down to the mattress, and they basked in languid afterglow kisses a few moments, but soon, the fever returned. Ross slid inside her once more, and Callie lost herself to feeling, happiness, excitement.

The night was quiet, but its loneliness was gone. Ross was with her, family was comfortingly near, and she knew she'd always be surrounded by love.

She gave the love back to him, this man of dark blue eyes and sinful smiles. Callie caught his kisses with hers as he began to move inside her, and surrendered herself to the man of her heart.

Epilogue

❧❧❧

W ell, that's one more Campbell married off."
Kyle Malory heard his brother's drawl as Ray stepped beside him, a longneck held in relaxed fingers.

Ray and Kyle looked to where Callie and Ross danced their first dance as man and wife. Ross had his hand on Callie's bared back, the pair two-stepping in perfect balance to the band's rollicking tune. Ross wore cowboy boots under his tux pants; Callie, satin slippers that went with her body-hugging white silk gown. No tulle in sight.

They looked like the perfect fairy-tale couple, Western style. Good for Ross, nabbing the best girl in town.

"The Malorys are gonna have to catch up," Ray said after a sip of beer.

"Grace is taking care of that for us," Kyle reminded him. "We're not all lonely losers."

"Speak for yourself. Grace married a Campbell, officially helping the rivals."

"A Sullivan." Kyle glanced to where Carter sat with Grace, their son on his lap, starry-eyed daughter at his side. "But you're right—Carter's a Campbell now. He got sucked in. So did Grace."

Grace wiped drool from baby Zach's mouth with a tissue and said something to Carter, laughing when Carter responded.

Kyle had never seen his sister look so happy. It made him warm and fuzzy inside, but that might just be the large number of beers he'd already consumed.

"Lucy is off being a businesswoman," Ray said. "So it's up to us to fill the house with kids."

Kyle turned his head to stare at his brother. "What's got you so sentimental? I thought only the ladies were teary-eyed at weddings."

Ray gazed at the couples joining the dance. "Getting older, I guess."

Adam and Bailey swung in. Then Grant and Christina. Carter and Grace, Carter still holding his son. Tyler and Jess. Olivia Campbell with the banker, Mr. Carew. *Hmm*, Kyle thought, narrowing his eyes.

Faith and Dominic danced too, twirling each other in playful imitation of the adults.

Kyle saw Manny Judd, cleaned up in a suit, shyly asking Deputy Harrison's younger sister, who was still in high school, to dance. Ross had really helped Manny, taking him under his wing.

The young woman returned Manny's smile, equally as shy, and let him lead her out. Harrison watched carefully, but didn't interfere or look like he disapproved.

Kyle felt eyes on him—not Ray, who was watching the dancing with a wistful look that bordered on maudlin.

Kyle turned his head and saw Anna Lawler's blue gaze fixed upon him.

She'd wound her braided blond hair around the crown of her head, which made her look a like an old-fashioned milk-maid. Instead of her usual jeans and work boots, she wore a satiny dress of dark blue that clung to her curves and bared a nice amount of leg.

Anna caught Kyle's stare and flushed a deep red, but she didn't look away, defiance in her eyes.

Kyle gave her a little nod, acknowledging that yes, he was staring at her. Anna held his gaze a while longer then coolly turned away. *Whatever,* her body language said.

"Huh."

Ray's grunt made Kyle jerk his attention from Anna. His brother's green eyes held mirth and a knowing look.

"What?" Kyle asked in irritation.

Ray pretended innocence, comical in a man as bulky and mean-looking as he was. "Nothing. I only said *huh*."

"Keep your *huhs* to yourself. I am not interested in Anna Lawler."

"If you say so."

Kyle snapped his mouth shut, knowing more words would only add fuel to Ray's fire.

The Campbell brothers smiled down at their wives, and their ladies wrapped arms around them, contented and obviously in love. How the hell did the dirtbag Campbells get so lucky?

Karen Marvin two-stepped very close to her cowboy of choice tonight, a young bull rider who couldn't be much above drinking age. Anna watched the dancing, tapping her foot in a petite, high-heeled shoe.

"Go on." Ray leaned to Kyle. "Ask her."

"You're a shit, Ray, you know that?"

"What's one dance going to hurt?" Ray asked, eyes sparkling. "You don't have to marry her."

That was true. Anna obviously wanted to dance, and Kyle was just standing there, so why not?

Kyle ignored Ray's rumbling laughter and wove through neighbors and friends to where Anna waited, her hair like gold fire, a question in her blue eyes.

Author's Note

Ross's story tells the final Happily Ever After of the Campbell brothers, but there's much more going on in Riverbend. Next comes the Malorys' stories — *Riding Hard: Kyle* and *Riding Hard: Ray*.

You might have guessed that Dr. Anna, the vet, will be the heroine of Kyle's book. I have someone special in mind for Ray — she will be introduced in Kyle's book. Lucy Malory will also return to Riverbend to find happiness in a way she did not expect.

I've enjoyed my foray into contemporary romance, and Western romance in particular. I've lived in the West most of my life (Texas, Arizona, Nevada), and it feels natural for me to write about horses, ranches, cowboys, and the laid-back Western way of life. Even in the heart of the cities, you don't forget you're in big country with huge skies and immense landscape. As much as I love to travel, I'm relieved when I see the vast spaces spreading out outside my window (be it train, car, or plane), and I know I'm home.

If you've never visited these states, take a trip, plan long drives, and soak up the beauty from the heart of Texas to the southwestern deserts, to the coastline of California. Just a warning, in the summer, this journey will be hot! Spring and fall, however, are absolutely beautiful.

See you back in Riverbend!

Jennifer Ashley

Also by Jennifer Ashley

Riding Hard

(Contemporary Romance)

Adam

Grant

Carter

Tyler

Ross

Kyle

Ray

Snowbound in Starlight Bend

Shifters Unbound

(Paranormal Romance)

Pride Mates

Primal Bonds

Bodyguard

Wild Cat

Hard Mated

Mate Claimed

"Perfect Mate" (novella)

Lone Wolf

Tiger Magic

Feral Heat

Wild Wolf

Bear Attraction

Mate Bond

Lion Eyes

Bad Wolf

Wild Things

White Tiger

Guardian's Mate

Red Wolf

Midnight Wolf

Tiger Striped (novella)

Shifter Made ("Prequel" short story)

Immortals

(Paranormal Romance)

The Calling (by Jennifer Ashley)

The Darkening (by Robin Popp)

The Awakening (by Joy Nash)

The Gathering (by Jennifer Ashley)

The Redeeming (by Jennifer Ashley)

The Crossing (by Joy Nash)

The Haunting (by Robin Popp)

Blood Debt (by Joy Nash)

Wolf Hunt (by Jennifer Ashley)

Forbidden Taste (by Jennifer Ashley)

About the Author

New York Times bestselling and award-winning author Jennifer Ashley has written more than 85 published novels and novellas in romance, urban fantasy, and mystery under the names Jennifer Ashley, Allyson James, and Ashley Gardner. Her books have been nominated for and won Romance Writers of America's RITA (given for the best romance novels and novellas of the year), several *RT BookReviews* Reviewers Choice awards (including Best Urban Fantasy, Best Historical Mystery, and Career Achievement in Historical Romance), and Prism awards for her paranormal romances. Jennifer's books have been translated into more than a dozen languages and have earned starred reviews in *Booklist*.

More about the Jennifer's books can be found at
http://www.jenniferashley.com.
Or join her newsletter at
http://eepurl.com/47kLL

Made in the USA
Monee, IL
26 July 2022